'He's what, thirty-o

'Thirty-two.'

'Mm. By that a ... r
seriously thinking a ... er
had a girlfriend tha ... 's
anything wrong wi

'I should hope not.'

'Oh far from it.'

'He's a proper man's man, our Colin.'

'Of course he is. You can tell them other kind a mile off, can't you? I wasn't suggesting anything like that, Ena. But it's unusual him never having anything to do with women, isn't it?'

By the same author

The Outsider
The Dark Side of the Sun

EastEnders Novels

Home Fires Burning
Swings and Roundabouts
Good Intentions
The Flower of Albert Square
Blind Spots
Hopes and Horizons
The Baffled Heart
Growing Wild
A Place in Life

HUGH MILLER

A Single Man

EastEnders – Book 10

By arrangement with the British Broadcasting Corporation

GRAFTON BOOKS
A Division of the Collins Publishing Group

LONDON GLASGOW
TORONTO SYDNEY AUCKLAND

Grafton Books
A Division of the Collins Publishing Group
8 Grafton Street, London W1X 3LA

A Grafton Paperback Original 1987

ISBN 0-586-07227-6

Printed and bound in Great Britain by
Cox & Wyman Ltd, Reading

Set in Times

1

On Fridays Ena Russell liked to go to her local Cataract Club in Ealing. She didn't go – as some of her neighbours supposed – to find comfort among people who suffered as she did and who could ease her distress by sharing their experiences and tips for making life easier; Ena's main solace on these visits came from the fact that the others were all much worse-off than she was.

'Blind as bats, most of them,' she would say. 'Kidding themselves they've come to terms and learned to cope, and all the time they're bumping into doors and into each other and spilling hot tea down their fronts.'

This Friday she was giving the Cataract Club a miss. Her sister-in-law, Joan, was coming over from Chiswick. Joan visited only once a month, so Ena always had to bring her up to date on what had been happening. Even if the news was thin, there were enough stories about Ena's health picture to take up an entire afternoon. Apart from the cataracts, which developed slowly and caused her hardly any trouble, her diabetes had produced other offshoots that distracted her in rotation throughout the day and gave her plenty of material for conversation. Illness had its advantages when it came to having a natter.

At half-past one, with her lunch over and the dishes sorted away, she decided there was time to see to her feet and her pins-and-needles before she got changed into a fresh dress to greet her sister-in-law.

Her poor circulation was tackled first. It was a challenge she answered by vigorously rubbing her hands and arms, three times a day, with a rough pad made from an old towel. The ritual took a carefully-timed ten minutes. When that was done Ena got out her special plastic basin and took it to the bathroom. Swollen ankles and aching joints were bathed in hot water and cosseted with powders, creams and ointments, applied in combinations and quantities that were governed, today as always, by the whim of the moment.

'There's days I can tell when one lot's going to do me more good than another,' she told people, whether they were interested or not. 'You get to know these things when you've been a martyr to bad feet as long as I have.'

When she had tended herself and put on the blue dress printed with large sprays of roses – the Sunday special her son called Floribunda – she dabbed 4711 on her wrists and behind her ears, patted her stiff grey hair without altering its shape or position, then sat down to wait for the doorbell to ring.

Joan arrived promptly at two-fifteen, as she always did. She invariably left at the same time, too; four forty-five, so she would be home in time to prepare tea for her daughter.

'You can see the changes in this street,' Joan said, as soon as she was settled in an armchair with coffee and a plate of biscuits on the little table beside her. 'Small things, but real obvious. And a lot of small things can add up to big changes, can't they?'

'I've never noticed much change,' Ena said.

'That's because you see the place all the time. It's like watching a kitten grow into a cat. To other people it seems to happen so fast, but because you're with it all the time the changes are so gradual you don't notice.' Joan, who bore a disconcerting resemblance to Alfie Bass, made a swift wrinkle of her nose and a pursing of her mouth that warned Ena she was about to say something unflattering. Joan did that before she mentioned certain relatives, or public figures, or present-day trends that offended her. 'The street just seems to be, I don't know, going down. It looks kind of scruffy nowadays.'

'It's still good enough for me.'

Ena said it without rancour. It was twenty-eight years since her husband had died; she'd bought the house soon afterwards from the insurance money and a little of her savings, and although it was a modest terrace dwelling without particular style or generosity of room-space, over the years it had made her feel secure and happy, or as happy as a widow could be with two sons to bring up on her own.

'I'm glad Elaine and me made the move when we did,' Joan said. 'I was beginning to see terrible changes down our road, too.'

Ena believed it might be time to launch an update of her medical history, before Joan got on to the topic of the home that she, too, had bought from the benefits of sudden widowhood. Ena's brother had died two years before, leaving Joan comfortable enough to move up a notch on the social scale – superficially, at any rate. The proportion of Tories to Socialists in her old district had always been sadly unbalanced, she felt; the pain of the situation grew deeper when Mrs Thatcher came to power in 1979 and Joan had to listen to her heroine being openly maligned and slandered by the neighbours. But all that was changed now, and Joan grabbed every opportunity to talk about her rise in the world.

'Whatever it is about the people where we live now,' she said, 'they seem to take more pride in their surroundings and look after them a lot better.'

Ena took her cue from a sudden drumming of raindrops on the window. 'My legs feel worse in this weather,' She leaned forward and rubbed her calf. 'I hope I'm not getting rheumatics on top of everything else.'

'How have you been lately anyway?' Joan asked. She didn't mind being diverted to a discussion of illness and ailments; she had been a nurse for a short time before her marriage, which made her – in her own view – a medical authority within her circle of relatives and friends. 'It's important to keep your head and feet dry at this time of year. Not enough people realize how vital that is.'

'I don't reckon it'd make much difference if I lagged myself,' Ena said. 'The diabetes seems to work out from the middle of my bones. Just lately the doctor's been giving me these . . .' She reached across to the tiled mantelpiece and took down a bottle of tablets. 'I don't know what they're supposed to do.' She handed them to Joan. 'The only difference I've noticed is that I feel a lot more bilious these days.'

Joan peered at the label, then held the bottle importantly to the window light.

'They'll be for your blood,' she said, handing them back.

'What are they supposed to do, exactly?'

'Well . . .' Joan frowned. 'It's hard to explain in layman's language. With a condition like yours there's a lot of extra sugar floating about in the blood. The tablets soak it up, so it can't do any harm.'

'I've never understood that,' Ena said, shaking her head.

'You're not supposed to, love. It's best left to the people that're trained to understand.'

'It's this sugar business, though,' Ena insisted. 'The doctor used a word when he talked about it. Hyper-gly-something-or-other. What's that when it's at home?'

Joan cleared her throat, playing for time. 'It's, ah, it's a way to describe what the sugar's *doing* to your system, actually.'

'And what's the word again? Hyper-gly . . .'

'It's one of the newer names. Hyperglycology. Too much sugar doing too much harm, that's what it means.'

'But I hardly ever eat sweet things. I don't even take sugar in my tea or coffee. So how can I have too much in my blood? Colin tried to explain it to me, but I got lost . . .'

'So how is Colin, anyway?' Joan asked, getting herself away from the tricky medical point.

'He's fine. Same as always. Steeped in his work most of the time, looking after me when he's not.' Ena smiled. 'He's always been a steady lad, our Colin. I keep wishing his dad could have been spared to see how he's turned out. Him and Bill both. I've been blessed with good sons.'

'No sign of a girlfriend yet?'

'None that I know of. It's like his brother says, I reckon – Colin's a natural-born bachelor.' They had had this conversation before. It was as if Joan had to bring it up at yearly intervals. 'Very self-contained, he is,' Ena added, for emphasis.

Joan made another face. It suggested she found Ena's answer less than satisfactory.

'Odd, isn't it, though?' she said. 'He's what, thirty-one?'

'Thirty-two.'

'Mm. By that age most men are either married or seriously thinking about it, aren't they? Yet Colin's never had a girlfriend that I know of. Not that I'm saying there's anything wrong with him.'

'I should hope not.'

'Oh far from it.'

'He's a proper man's man, our Colin.'

'Of course he is. You can tell them other kind a mile off, can't you? I wasn't suggesting anything like that, Ena. But it's unusual him never having anything to do with women, isn't it?'

Ena shrugged. 'Folk look at things a different way nowadays. I mean in our day getting married was something a man did whether he was set up in life or not. Colin's generation are a bit more cautious. They put first things first. Security, then marriage. That's what somebody was saying on the box the other night and I have to say it fits Colin's case to a tee. He's done well in his work, he's put a fair few pounds in the bank and the building society. He's spent his time and energy making himself secure. He might well be thinking about getting married now, for all I know. But then again, he *does* have that self-contained thing about him. It's hard to pin down, but some chaps just have it.'

'I suppose so,' Joan said, letting the doubt linger in her voice. 'It seems kind of sad, somehow. A man's not complete without a wife, is he? And there's the other thing, of course . . .'

'What?'

'You know,' Joan averted her eyes, as she usually did on the threshold of delicate matters. 'People have their needs, don't they? It's nature. There's got to be an outlet.'

'Sex, you mean.'

'Well . . .'

'That's Colin's own business,' Ena said flatly. 'He's a placid chap. Who's to say he's bothered with that kind of thing? He's wrapped up in his work, maybe it's enough for him.'

'Yes, maybe,' Joan said, the doubt hovering in her tone again. 'It's a pity people don't realize that more, instead of gossiping the way they do.'

'Gossiping?'

'About single men past a certain age. Saying how odd it is, them being on their own. It's very unfortunate, I always think. Very unfair.'

'Yes.' Ena's jaw tensed for a second. 'And what about your Elaine?'

Joan frowned. 'How do you mean?'

'How is she?'

'Oh. She's happy and prospering,' Joan said tightly. 'As ever.'

'I saw on telly where the teachers are complaining they don't get enough pay. There's been demonstrations – I wondered if your Elaine was mixed up in that business, at all.'

Joan shook her head. 'She wouldn't have anything to do with them. She doesn't hold with the protests – she's perfectly content with her salary, anyway. They should all be, instead of letting a bunch of ban-the-bomb types and other left-wingers lead them like sheep.'

'And she's quite happy to stay single, I suppose,' Ena said, pointedly enough. 'It's like I was saying. For some people their work is enough.'

'Exactly,' Joan snapped.

'No matter what people say about old maids and the like,' Ena added, then pointed to Joan's cup. 'Would you like some more coffee?'

At four thirty-five, approximately the time his aunt would be making moves to get her coat on and go back to Chiswick, Colin Russell was arriving at two decisions. One was automatic and scarcely important – he would finish at half-past five tonight, instead of six as he usually did. The other decision was momentous. He was going to give up his job with Crabtree Ellis Associates and go freelance.

It was a heady sensation, sitting there at his drawing board and realizing he would soon be a free man. Free to work harder than ever before, free to struggle single-handed against the competition, and free to get bogged down in the paperwork and red tape connected with self-employment. But free, for all that. The decision had been delayed for months. Taking it, in the end, had been easy.

'You've got that look again,' Mandy Riley said as she came in with a pile of rolled drawings and dropped them on his desk.

'What look?'

'The one like a dog that's been let in out of the rain.' Mandy sat down, brushing a wisp of blonde hair from her forehead. 'You had it not long ago – the day you landed the private contract with Beverley's. It made quite a contrast to Mr Crabtree's look when *he* heard about the contract.'

Colin smiled. 'What did he look like, then?'

'A man with an ulcer.'

'Well, he does have an ulcer.'

'I know,' Mandy said. 'But that time it really showed.' She pulled forward a drawing, unrolled it, then looked at Colin again. 'What's the reason for the glad-puppy appearance, then? Or is it a secret?'

'For now, it's a secret,' Colin said. 'But when I do let it out, you'll be the first to know.' She would be the second to know. He was going to tell George when he met him in the pub after work. But Mandy would be the first one at work to know. Mr Crabtree would be next.

'I hate knowing there's a secret I'm not in on,' Mandy complained. 'How long do I have to wait?'

'A week or two.'

'Oh, God. A week or two. A day or two can be torture.' She stared at the drawing, a gouache of an old man tying a feather fly to a fishing hook. 'This secret better be worth my suffering.' With a soft-lead pencil she put a caption at the bottom of the picture for the lettering artist to copy. 'Can't you give me a clue to chew over?' She pleaded with her eyes and downcast mouth, tilting her head at Colin. 'What's one little clue going to hurt?'

'No clues.' Colin got off his stool and unclipped the drawing he had been finishing. He held it up. 'What do you think?'

Mandy tilted her head further, examining the picture. Colin had drawn a pair of chopsticks, crossing the paper diagonally with a glittering micro-chip caught between their tips.

'Nice, Colin. Nice. Not great, mind you. Not even exceptional. Not particularly talented or innovative, either, and I can't say – '

'Fine,' Colin interrupted, rolling up the picture. 'I'll settle for nice. Your "nice" is on a level with Crabtree's "highly imaginative". He's not as picky as you.'

Outside Mr Crabtree's door Colin had another look at the drawing, convincing himself it was all right. The promotion wasn't a major one, but he didn't want to give the impression he was under-valuing his part in the project. Of all his obsessions, the strongest was his desire, always, to provide more than was expected of him. The door opened while he was re-rolling the picture.

'Oh, Mr Crabtree. Do you have a minute?'

The senior partner shrugged. 'I was only going for a pee. A minute longer won't hurt me. Not much more than a minute, though.' He stepped back letting Colin into the office. 'I suspect I've got a blown prostate. You've heard about surprise pees? I've had a few near things. Sit down.'

Crabtree was overweight and invariably dishevelled. Today, in shirtsleeves and scuffed corduroy trousers, his wire-wool hair teased out in crinkly clumps and his chin darkening with stubble, he looked particularly frowzy. He shuffled over to the desk and sat down with a grunt.

'So. What have you brought me?'

'The Hao-Wan Electronics promotion,' Colin said,

unrolling the picture again and spreading it on the desk. 'I thought this would be just the thing for the brochure cover.'

Crabtree gazed at the drawing for a few seconds, then nodded at it. 'Nifty idea. I like it. Smooth execution, too. In fact it's more than the slit-eyed, tight-fisted little buggers deserve.' He nodded at the drawing again and slid it towards Colin. 'Get some colour reductions done and I'll send them round to their sweatshop. We'll throw in Davidson's ridiculous idea with the dragon made out of chips and resistors, just to let them see we've been putting in some effort.'

'Right. I'll get on to it.' Colin stood up.

'One thing, while you're here.' Crabtree tapped a fat plastic ring-binder lying on the desk. 'Hempel Cosmetics,' he said, his voice hushed with respect. 'We've closed a deal with them. Nationwide campaign. Colour spreads. Point-of-sale material. And it'll be high production values all the way – they're getting Duffy-Barton to do all the printing. This is one promo that can only do us good.'

'Congratulations,' Colin said.

'Thank you. But I wasn't bragging about my talent for bringing in accounts. How would you like to lead this one, Colin? Concepts, layouts, principal illustrations – the up-front works. Practically your own show. We've got six months to put it all together. What do you say?'

'Well, that's very kind.' Colin stroked his forehead, as he often did when he confronted a dilemma. 'I'm flattered, but I'm not sure I'm up to something like this.'

'Bullshit. Of course you're up to it. It's *you*. Tailor-made for your style. And remember, your name won't get submerged when the whole thing's off the board and running. There'll be credit given where it's due. You'll be doing your career a bit of good.'

'Don't you think Charlie Winton's the man for this

one? He's done big promotions before, and he's closer to the cosmetic side, isn't he?'

'He's flat, Colin. Flat. Stale. He's been doing cosmetic ads so long he's got into a rut.' Crabtree tapped his chest. 'My fault, I'll admit that. I shouldn't have let him get that way. But that's not the point at issue here. The point is, Colin, that *I* know you're the man for the Hempel account, even if you don't believe it yourself. Ten minutes ago I decided I was going to put you on to this one. What you've just shown me confirms my decision. You're the bloke. Period.'

Colin started to say something but Crabtree stopped him.

'Just go away and think about it, eh? Get your head behind the concept of a large-scale hustle. Face the thing instead of thinking up reasons why it's beyond you.' Crabtree stood up. 'I want you to do it, but I want you to do it in the right frame of mind. Here . . .' He picked up the binder and gave it to Colin. 'Take that away and study it. See what the SP is and measure it against your own flair. If you give it the right amount of thought and still don't think it's for you, well . . .' He shrugged. 'I'll be very sorry.'

'Right,' Colin murmured. 'I'll look it over and have a think. But really, I don't think – '

'Not another word,' Crabtree said, striding to the door. 'Come and see me on Monday morning and we'll talk about it again. Meanwhile, if I don't have that pee right now there'll be a very squalid accident.'

Back in his own office Colin put the ring binder on his stool and stared at it. Mandy watched him for a minute then cleared her throat loudly.

'Is there some danger of that thing biting you?' she asked.

Colin sighed. 'It's a little tragedy, Mandy. A promotion I'd have given one of my toes for, a year or two ago.

Crabtree's just dropped it in my lap. Hempel Cosmetics.'

'So why aren't you cheering?'

'I can't do it.'

Mandy stared at him. 'How come? Are you suffering a crisis of talent, or something?'

'I don't have the time.' Colin turned to Mandy and spread his hands. 'That secret of mine – you won't have to wait a week or two after all. I'll tell you now. I'm leaving.'

She looked genuinely shocked.

'You touched on my reason a few minutes ago. You know the arrangement I have here – I can take on private projects as long as there's no question of poaching from the firm, and as long as private work doesn't interfere with the time I'm obliged to spend here.' Colin moved the binder and sat on the stool. 'Lately, for a year, say, I've been handling more and more private jobs. Without touting for them. Word of mouth's been good.'

'Are you talking about going freelance?'

Colin nodded.

'Christ, that's a bit risky. It's tooth-and-claw country out there.'

'I know. That's why I haven't considered moving, until now. Well, until a couple of months ago. I've been getting some very good commissions, Mandy. They've been threatening to eat into my time here. A decision had to be made, sooner or later. So, when the managing director of Mason and Gilchrist got on to me this afternoon and offered me the biggest private commission I've had yet, I made up my mind. I was going to tidy up all the ends here before I put in my notice, so I wouldn't leave Crabtree Ellis in a bind.' Colin pointed at the binder. 'Then Crabtree hands me that. The two best jobs I've been offered, both on the same day. And I've got to turn the better one down.'

'Have you told the boss that?'

'No. He bulldozed me a bit. But I'll have to tell him on Monday. God . . .' Colin rubbed his eyes with flattened fingers. 'I don't know whether to laugh or cry.'

Mandy studied her fingernails. 'On balance,' she said, 'I think you should be laughing.' She looked at Colin. 'You've got it made. You've always wanted to be an independent, haven't you? Running your own show . . .'

'I'll miss this place. I've had some good years here.'

'The place'll miss you.' Mandy stood up. '*I'll* miss you. We've been sharing this rat trap of an office for eighteen months. I've almost come to feel I'm living with you.'

'Oh, there's been a certain amount of domestic harmony between us,' Colin said, grinning. 'Have you noticed the way one of us or the other will always go round straightening the place if somebody else has been in and disordered this or that? You're going to have to do the housework on your own, from now on.'

'Until my new partner moves in,' Mandy said glumly. 'Jesus. I hope it's somebody I can live with. Otherwise you'll have a caption writer on the blower begging you for a job.'

Colin looked round the room. Leaving its familiar confines would be quite a jolt. He had generated a lot of ideas in here and seen them through to finished artwork. It had been the scene of small triumphs and the occasional flop. He glanced at his reproduction Mondrian on the wall beside the door, a gift from Mandy, then looked at the sign she had tacked above her own desk:

I KNOW YOU BELIEVE YOU UNDERSTAND WHAT I SAID, BUT I'M NOT SURE YOU REALISE THAT WHAT YOU HEARD WASN'T WHAT I MEANT.

'Partings,' Colin said. 'I hate them. I never seem to remember arrivals very clearly. Only the leaving. Being separated from something or somebody . . .'

Mandy came across and pecked his cheek. 'Think of this as an arrival. You've arrived where you always wanted to be. You've taken the big step at exactly the right time.'

'Yes, you're right,' he said softly, wondering what George would say when he told him.

2

'What do you mean?' a camel-coated man at the bar demanded.

'I think I made it nice and clear.' The barman was a dark-haired youth whose voice was a great deal harder than his eyes. 'You've had enough. You should go out and get some air about you.'

'An excess of anything I like still isn't enough for me,' the man said. He pushed back his bowler hat and winked at the barman. 'I may look as if I've had enough. I may *sound* as if I'm pissed. But everything's relative, my friend. I mean, compared to that feller in the corner, him talking to his briefcase, I'm as sober as an advocate. Let's not quibble, eh? Another large scotch in there and a gin and frolic for my friend.'

'Well try not to knock it all over the counter this time,' the barman said. He picked up the glasses and walked away.

'Sweet enough lad,' the man said to his companion. 'He just gets surly with the pressure. He should work somewhere more restful.'

Behind them George Packer was trying to catch the eye of the landlord. He had been there for over a minute and by now his impatience was like a force-field round him, making other punters move aside without being pressed. When finally the corpulent guv'nor turned from a conversation with his wife George's hand shot up. He delivered his order in a strident, RADA-trained voice.

'Two pints of bitter, please. If it's not too much trouble.'

The landlord considered what George had said, then beckoned him close to the bar with a curled finger.

'What do you mean, "if it's not too much trouble"?' He demanded. 'Was that some kind of wisecrack?'

'Read it any way you like,' George said.

'Listen.' The landlord lowered his head very slowly, a movement that said a lot about his self-possession. 'If you're goin' to come on with the heavy patter, you better get yourself a minder. The fact I let you in here doesn't mean you can treat the place like you owned it. Under this roof you'll show a bit of civility to me an' the rest of the staff. Got it?'

George swallowed, trying not to let it show. The landlord's face was set hard, requiring an answer before the transaction could go any further. Even so, George didn't think he should climb down.

'You're over-reacting,' he heard himself say.

'An' you're tremblin' like a dog shittin' whipcord, so don't come the cool smoothie with *me*, son.' One fat hand slapped the bar with dull finality. 'I've handed you a little warnin'. Now I'm waitin' to hear if you got it.'

George shuffled his feet, aware others were listening. 'I've got it,' he mumbled.

'Fine.' The landlord picked up a glass and turned to the pumps. 'Two pints it is, then.'

Sorting through his loose change and affecting as much casualness as he could, George saw, from the corner of his eye, that two men on his left were looking at him and murmuring to each other. That happened a lot since he'd done the aftershave commercial. People stared, or asked each other where they'd seen that face before. There was also his close resemblance – well, George believed it was close – to Michael Douglas. For lots of little physical reasons he drew people's attention wherever he went. Even at a moment like this, stinging from the landlord's impudence, George found it soothing that his appearance should have such power to arrest the flow of other people's business.

By the time he got to the table with the drinks, after squeezing through huddle after huddle of dark-suited commuters, a good half-inch of beer had been spilled from each glass. George's knuckles were dripping.

'Sodding place,' he snapped, banging down the drinks. 'I don't know why I bother coming in.'

Colin drew his glass towards him, wiping the froth off the sides with his fingers. 'Agents use it,' he said. 'And one or two showbiz biggies. That's why you come in. You're keeping yourself in the market place, remember?'

'Not at this time of night, I'm not.' George flung himself into the chair opposite Colin. He waved a hand at the nearest group of businessmen. 'Look at them. Quiet desperation masquerading as noisy jollity. They can't wait to get in here and stun themselves before they go home to face their hideous wives and ghastly kids and their midnight terrors. Christ.'

'There, there, it'll be better later on,' Colin said, grinning. 'The sparkling people will be in. You'll be able to relax then. You're always at your best in the presence of the glitterati.'

George rearranged himself in the chair, propping one denimed knee on the edge of the table and easing down until he was able to look at Colin with his chin resting on his chest.

'Glitterati?' He made a sour mouth. 'Shitterati, more like. This boozer isn't what it was. The prime movers have moved on, if you ask me. The clientele has turned small-beer, as I'm sure you've noticed.'

Colin shrugged. 'Maybe you're just getting above it all. Seeing through your inferiors – now you know they're inferior.'

George swallowed a mouthful of beer and scowled. He did it a muscle at a time, letting the effect build. 'I can't make up my mind,' he said, 'if you're flattering me, giving me the picture straight, or taking the piss. What's with you tonight? You're animated. Almost. Has something happened?'

'Yes.'

'Am I to be told about it?'

Colin nodded.

'So tell me, then.'

'I'm packing in the job.'

'Never.' George sat forward. 'What the hell are you doing that for?'

'You know I've wanted to, for ages. I've decided to stop wanting and get around to achieving. I'm a free man. Or I will be soon.'

'But can you afford to do it?'

'I can't afford not to. I'm in demand, George. I've got to the point where if I don't go on my own full time, I'll have to turn work away. And I'd be crazy to do that.'

'Well, well . . .'

George was trying to look impressed, but what showed was displeasure. Other people's success or progress irritated him if it tended, as this news did, to highlight his own professional shortfalls.

'It's not going to be a doddle,' Colin said. 'Being self-employed never is. But I'm prepared to work hard, day and night if I have to. And I won't even be considering failure as an alternative.'

'That's got a familiar ring.' George smiled thinly. 'It's practically the standard fanfare to disaster.'

Colin looked around the room, watched a man lean his chair too far back and have to be caught by two other men standing behind him. He looked at George again.

'You don't think I'm making the right move, then.'

'I didn't say that.' George took a gulp from his glass. 'For all I know, you're doing precisely the right thing. But I've seen a lot of people go down the plumbing just because they thought a patch of good luck was the dawn of a new era in their lives.'

'I've tested the water over a long period,' Colin said. 'There's nothing precipitate about what I'm doing. I've been planning it. Carefully.'

'You never told me about any plans.'

'You knew I wanted to go independent . . .'

'Oh, sure, I knew it in a general way. I knew you harboured the ambition.' George sniffed and drummed his fingers on the table. 'I wasn't let in on any *plans*. Only the real intimates get the lowdown on anything that important, I suppose.'

'Oh come on, George . . .'

'I'm not complaining, Colin. I don't go around assuming I've any rights where you're concerned.'

'Of course you've got rights – and you're entitled to know when something important happens in my life. You're the first person I've told about this . . .' Colin hesitated. 'Well, almost the first. I did tell somebody else, to clarify matters.'

'Let me guess. Little Mandy, the Doris Day clone?'

'Yes,' Colin said. 'As a matter of fact it was Mandy. She's a colleague and in the circumstances I felt she had a right to be put in the picture. My decision will affect her, after all.'

'I'll bet.' George sullenly flipped a beer mat across the table.

Colin leaned forward. 'George, what is it?'

These dips in George's mood weren't new, but they were on the increase. Colin knew that insecurity played a big part, but knowing it didn't help. George couldn't seem to take and keep the reassurances Colin regularly handed him.

'Everything just seems to be turning to shit.'

Colin stared, remembering something. 'Your audition. My God, I forgot.'

'Well . . .' George made a vague, dismissive gesture. 'You had important things on your mind. Big plans and so forth.'

'How did it go?'

'It didn't. It was a non-starter. The part was filled two days ago. My bloody agent again. Men living in monasteries are better informed than he is.'

'Oh, George, I'm sorry – really I am. You wanted that part, didn't you?'

'I want any part.' George sighed. 'Unlike your illustrious self, I haven't exactly been snowed-under with offers. I've another audition next week. Maybe I'll do better then.'

Colin nodded, thinking as he had again and again since he'd known George, that an actor's existence must be hell at times. In the past year George had been in work for a total of nine weeks, and there were others worse off than that. In a world where there was plenty of other work to do in the meantime, until a part turned up, the actor's existence wasn't so bad. There wasn't much time for a man or woman to contemplate just how little stage and television work there was, or ever would be. But George couldn't get any other kind of work. Not in London in 1984. Perhaps not anywhere in Britain, given his temperament and the general work drought. He had too many hours a day, too many days a week to dwell on his situation.

'I feel like a berk,' Colin said. 'I mean, you'd give just about anything for a job. Today you had your hopes crashed for the umpteenth time and you're feeling really down. Then I waltz in, me with my safe, well-paid job – and I announce I'm chucking it up. No wonder you're edgy.'

'Well . . .' George shrugged. 'It always hurts a bit to take somebody's good news on board when my own landscape's so bleak. And the nature of your news, in the circumstances, is a bit galling. But in a couple of hours I'll have what you told me in perspective.' He raised his glass. 'Although I don't quite feel like it, something sensible at my centre tells me congratulations are in order.'

They clinked their glasses and drained them.

'Another one?' Colin said, half-rising.

'No. I've decided I'm not staying tonight.'

'Oh.' Colin looked disappointed. 'Going somewhere special?'

'Might do. I haven't made up my mind what I'm doing – except that I'm not stopping here. It depresses me.'

So they would be changing their drinking haunt again, Colin thought. He had known George for eight months. In that time, always because of a whim of George's, they had changed their 'local' at roughly six-weekly intervals. George explained his restlessness by pointing out that he wasn't restless at all. It was simply that Colin, being an older man, had become fixed in his ways.

'I reckon I'll hang on for a while, George. Always like to get a couple or three pints inside me on a Friday night before I go home.'

'Yeah. It gives you time to suss out the talent too, I suppose. That way you might not have to go home at all.'

Colin sat down again. 'That wasn't fair, George. I know you're feeling rough, but you don't have to take it out on me.' This was all wrong, he thought. He'd wanted tonight to be carefree, a time for good-natured celebration. But George was on a short fuse. 'Have another drink and try to relax, eh?'

George was staring off far to his left, towards the bar. 'That barman, the semi-mediterranean one – he's got quite a smouldery look about him, hasn't he?'

Now he's trying to make me jealous, Colin thought.

'I mean,' George went on, 'he has a sort of compressed energy, you know? Under control, but only just.'

'Maybe he's got heartburn.' Colin picked up his empty glass. 'Are you having another drink, or what?'

'No.' George stood up smartly. 'I'm cutting.' He pushed back his chair and moved away from the table. 'Have a nice weekend, huh?'

'What about tomorrow?' Colin said.

'What about it?'

'We were supposed to be going out for a bite.'

'Oh.' George enacted recollection and sudden regret. 'I forgot. I've gone and made other plans.' He spread his hands. 'Sorry.' His hands dropped, slapping his jeans. 'I'll be in touch some time. OK? See you.'

'Right,' Colin sighed. 'See you.'

He watched George swagger off and wondered if he was only, in the end, a focus for that young man's frustration and spite. Getting up and taking his glass to the bar, he formed the tight-lipped hope that his news – and his presence, for that matter – would get a better reception from his mother.

'Joan was saying she thought this street was going down a bit,' Ena said, for all the world as if she were addressing the fireplace directly. 'I told her it's still good enough for me.'

This was the taking-it-in time, Colin knew. He wondered if his father had ever understood this woman the way he did. She was an elaborate series of responses to life, a network of defences and assaults backed by some awareness that she was a hub. Ena didn't like it when her sense of order was disturbed. Her often repeated line, *My family are everything to me,* really meant, *My family revolves around me, and I do all I can to keep it that way.* Colin's news, he realized, represented some threat to Ena's notion of the way things should be. Just how severe the threat was, she wasn't yet sure. She was filling the taking-it-in time with idle, disjointed comments on her day, until her mind made itself up.

'I'm going to poach myself a couple of eggs and make some toast, Mum. Do you fancy anything?'

'I shouldn't eat too much late at night,' she said, still hunched forward in her chair, staring at the fire.

'It's only nine o'clock.'

'Maybe some toast, then. With marmalade. Make sure it's the diabetic stuff, on the second shelf.'

Colin went into the kitchen and turned on one ring of the cooker. He filled the kettle and a saucepan with water and shook vinegar into the pan, then set it on the hot ring. When eggs, bread, butter and marmalade had been set out he switched on the kettle. Timing was everything in the kitchen. By the time the eggs began to poach the kettle would be boiled; the tea would be nicely infused when the last two slices popped out of the toaster. Colin had it down to a neat routine.

Ena came into the kitchen as he was breaking the second egg into the bubbling pan. Here it comes, Colin thought. The news had set in and she would now deliver judgement.

'I think you're making the wrong decision, Colin.' She sat down at the pine-topped breakfast table. 'Wrong altogether. In this day and age a job's a precious thing – it always was, come to that. But now especially.'

'I'll have a job, Mum. I just won't be doing it for some other company. I'll be doing it for myself.'

'But where's the sense? You're looked after at that

place. Look at all the benefits you've got, and all you have to do is go in five days a week and do your work.'

Colin created a gentle whirlpool on top of the water, watching the eggs, yellowy blobs trailing white tendrils as they revolved. 'I've explained it all,' he said. 'I can make a lot more money working on my own. I'll have much more creative freedom, too. Bags of flexibility in every direction. It's what I've been working for, all this time. It's not just some rash notion I've had.'

'Security, Colin. Where's the security in working for yourself?'

'My reputation's my security.'

Ena slapped the table impatiently. 'That's just words. What's really happened is you've got above yourself.'

'Aw, Mum, for any sake . . .'

'One or two people got you to do jobs privately. You've let that swell your head. You think you're better than the people that've given you a living all this time.'

'I'm sorry you see things that way.' Colin poured boiling water into the teapot and put on the lid. 'I'll say it one more time, just for the record. I'm going into business on my own because I can't afford not to.'

'What nonsense . . .'

'The people I work for now – how do you think they started out? Two freelancers, that's what they were. They put that firm together from talents that had flourished on independence. Before they had their independence they served their time working for other people. I'm only doing what a lot of men and women in my line do. There's a proper direction to my career, I'm not breaking any rules or going against the grain.'

Ena sighed. 'It seems too sudden, somehow. Irresponsible . . .'

Colin's timing had been upset. He'd forgotten the toast. Cursing soundlessly he put the eggs on a plate and slipped it in the top chamber of the cooker to keep warm. He flung two slices of bread into the toaster and thrust down the plunger. Then he turned to his mother.

'Sudden, you say? Haven't you watched the way I've built up that room upstairs, item by item, making it into a professional working space? I could turn round first thing tomorrow and start work on *any* project up there. That's taken me years to create, Mum, but it's been done with one goal in mind, and I've never deviated from that goal. Now I've achieved it. You should be pleased for me, instead of complaining that I'm irresponsible.'

They had their supper in silence. When it was over Colin took the cups, plates and cutlery to the kitchen and washed up. When he came back to the living room his mother had turned on the television set. She was watching a debate, which meant she wasn't watching at all. She was letting Colin know she was in a huff with him. He crossed to her chair, kissed her on the cheek and told her not to stay up too late. Upstairs he went into his studio and turned on the drawing-board lamp. Long shadows spread across the floor and walls. Colin closed the door and stood still, taking it in.

Why did people spoil things? This blessed space meant so much to him and tonight, of all times, it should have sung at him, welcoming him over to independence. Instead, he stood there uneasy and dispirited. Was it, maybe, that he didn't have the stuff of independence about him, and his mother was trying to tell him that? George, too?

They could have something. Colin had his problems when it came to asserting himself. That had always been the case. So did he perhaps misjudge his talent for business? There would be more to life from now on. It wouldn't simply be a matter of executing his layouts and drawings and leaving the commerce of it all to other men in other rooms. He would have to deal with people, argue with them, negotiate. He would have to hustle.

'Why now?' he murmured.

Why the doubts? They hadn't been there a week or a month ago. The answer was simple, he supposed – he was letting other people get him down. Specifically, two people who meant a great deal to him. And for their own reasons, perhaps, they were misleading him. George because he was insecure and occasionally very spiteful. Ena because . . .

'God, yes . . .'

He recalled now, with blazing clarity, what his mother had said a couple of weeks ago, talking on the 'phone to his older brother, Bill.

All them that are on the scrap heap now, calling themselves self-employed. It's just a posh way of being down and out. It fools nobody. I can still hold my head up. I've got two sons that are in proper jobs and doing well. Self-employed, indeed . . .

Colin smiled tightly, remembering something else, straight from the sharp tongue of George Packer: *If there's one thing women want, more than anything else in life, it's visible status.*

His mother no less than any other woman, Colin thought. The trouble was that he'd upset her sense of the way things should be, just as he'd suspected before supper – before he'd let his own misgivings make him think differently.

Oh, it was so obvious! He pictured her discomfort, half in pity, half in amusement. What would she tell the neighbours? That Colin was working from home nowadays? There were half a dozen men on the street working from home. Men collecting the dole and running very small-time businesses on the side. Ena didn't want Colin lumped with them, did she? And he would be, of course.

Her neighbours were as smart as she was. They weren't fooled that easily . . .

So much for his mother's objections. And George's? Just spite, Colin decided. Half-hearted spite, at that, for apart from anything else he'd said, he had offered his congratulations.

Colin went and sat at the drawing board. There was a single blank sheet of paper clipped there, stark white and full of potential. He uncapped a felt pen and held it over the centre of the paper for a second, then wrote, in confident red capitals, THE FUTURE STARTS HERE.

Right here, at this board, with inspiration and skill flooding from him, with energy and talent putting down a foundation that would steady him for life.

'The future starts here,' he whispered, giving it the assertion of speech as he underlined the words with a broad sweep of the pen.

If he chose to be really objective about his future, of course, he would have to accept that it was a leap into the dark. But wasn't that exhilarating, especially since the dark had already been pretty well mapped and plumbed. There would be unexpected obstacles, but a man who accepted challenges welcomed obstructions. They gave a challenge substance. They made it worthwhile.

'Don't worry, Mum,' Colin murmured, re-capping his pen. 'I'll see you stay proud of me.'

And as for George, he thought, getting off the stool and turning out the lamp, his little bouts of malice wouldn't dent this upsurge of self-confidence. Not very much, anyway.

3

In the second week of December, one month after Crabtree Ellis Associates bade a reluctant farewell to Colin Russell, there was another resignation that further saddened the old firm. Mandy Riley, never quite the same since Colin's departure, was offered a job in a publisher's office and decided to accept. Because of the time of year, Crabtree Ellis decided to waive the usual one month's notice and let Mandy go at once, so she could settle in at her new position before the New Year. An informal farewell party was organized in the Fir Tree, a pub near the office, and at Mandy's request Colin was invited.

He arrived twenty minutes late, red-faced and flustered. A drink was put in his hand and old colleagues gathered round, keen to know how he was doing.

'If I'd another pair of hands I'd open in Birmingham,' he told Mandy when finally they got to talk to each other. 'I've never been so busy in my life. Not ever.'

'I'm pleased for you,' she said. 'Another year and you'll be established. That's what they say, anyway. Get into your second year, still in profit, and you're made.'

'I hope they're right, whoever they are. But yes . . .' Colin nodded slowly, looking round at all the old faces, 'I think it's going to work. I can feel the business generating more business. People are looking at my work and thinking about what they'll ask me to do next. But enough of my blossoming career. What about you? How come you're leaving so soon after I did?'

'Charlie Winton,' Mandy said, lowering her voice. Winton was standing a couple of yards away. 'They moved him in with me. With you gone I was feeling restless enough. As soon as he arrived I got claustrophobia on top of everything else.'

'Yes, he can be difficult,' Colin said.

'Difficult? Listen, he's bizarre. Grotesque. He mumbles endlessly to himself while he's working. He picks his nose when he thinks. And he's inclined to talk dirty, in an oblique way. I think he has problems at home.'

'He lives with his mother.' Colin winced and added, 'Just like me.'

'He's nothing like you.'

'I'm relieved you think so.'

'He's always trying to help. That's another pain. Tells me he has a knack for caption writing and he never stops trying to prove it.' Mandy did an eye-roll. 'Apart from the fact his stuff was terrible, I always got the feeling he was trying to trespass on my responsibilities.'

'Oh, he would,' Colin assured her. 'But I'll tell you something about that – it's a piece of wisdom I've picked up in my long, disturbing experience of life. The answer to anybody who wants to lay claim to your responsibilities is to leave them to him. In the end you come out winning.'

'I'll write that down,' Mandy promised, 'then I'll get my auntie to embroider it and I'll stick it above my new desk.'

'Looking forward to the new job, are you?'

'Definitely. Either that, or I'm looking forward to life without Winton.' Mandy glanced aside as someone moved away from a knot of people by the bar. 'Oh heck,' she groaned. 'He's coming over.'

Colin watched the shambling approach, getting the impression he always had when he saw Winton – here was a man with no awareness of how he looked. He endlessly criticized other people for their manner or appearance, never realizing that he was a walking muddle of wrinkled clothes, unwashed greasy hair and bad attitudes, a person who made the senior partner, Crabtree, appear tidy and conventional by comparison.

'So the renegade's back amongst us,' Winton growled, slapping Colin's shoulder. He winked at Mandy. 'Come to pinch some ideas, has he? Pick a few brains, maybe?'

'I'm here to wish Mandy good luck,' Colin said. 'How have you been, Charlie?'

'Happier, for a while. But now my little dove here is flying the coop.' Winton looked at Mandy with something that might have been fondness. 'I was just getting to know her better, too.'

'All good things have to end,' Mandy said, forcing the brightness. 'Just as well we parted before the bond became too strong, Charlie. And you never know, they may move somebody new and appealing in beside you after Christmas.'

He shook his head. 'Not a chance. Now I've got that office to myself I'm hanging on to it. I need all the space I can get.' He offered Colin a crumpled smile. 'I'm doing the Hempel Cosmetics account, you know. Quite a feather in the titfer, wouldn't you say?'

'Congratulations,' Colin said. 'I'm sure you'll do a good job.'

In the old days, that remark would have been tagged with a thought like, *Not as good as I'd have done though, mate*. But not now. Colin had only been back among the crowd for minutes, yet already he realized that a lot of unpleasant habits and instincts had left him, swiftly, since he'd left Crabtree Ellis. The corporate bitching, the flimsy, shifting loyalties, the automatic damning of other people's work and the endless involvement in this or that petty faction – all of it had vanished, like the muck from a reformed smoker's lungs. Going independent had been a far more cleansing experience than Colin had expected.

'And how are you doing out there in the cold world?' Winton asked. 'Making a bob?'

'Surviving nicely, thanks.'

Winton fished something from his dental plate with his tongue. 'Never fancied that, myself. You can't beat the security of a good firm around you.'

'Or the deadening monotony, or the erosion of your talent,' Colin said, smiling to soften it and wondering if his bitchiness had disappeared after all. He decided he was being re-infected and swore, not too seriously, to make this his last reunion. 'Every bloke to what suits him, eh, Charlie?'

'S'pose so. But mind you . . .'

While Winton was mustering another banality Crabtree shuffled up, rosy from drink. He beamed at Colin.

'You're looking prosperous, damn you. How many of our clients have you poached, so far?'

'Dozens,' Colin said. 'You'll notice the difference in the New Year.'

'We've had our winter's tale already, thanks very much.' Crabtree closed an arm round Mandy's shoulder. 'I'd kind of fancied she'd grow old with us. But it wasn't to be.' He narrowed an eye at Colin. 'You're not behind her defection, are you? Tempting her away with stories of wider vistas beyond, or lies about better prospects on Grub Street, that kind of thing?'

'As if I would,' Colin grinned, recalling now the better things about his old job – the steady humour, the warmth of some people . . .

As Crabtree released Mandy she linked her arm in Colin's. 'The fact is,' she said, 'we're founder members of the Crabtree Ellis escape committee. You might as well know this gathering tonight is a recruitment rally.'

At that moment something entirely unexpected happened. George Packer appeared behind Crabtree. He was dressed in his best grey leathers, his hands hooked casually in the jacket pockets. Colin stared, caught off-guard as George stared back, taking in the tableau. Mandy eased her arm away from Colin's.

'So there you are,' George drawled. 'I called your place and your mother told me you were at a party here. I'd no idea it would be anything so jolly.'

Colin felt himself blush as he stepped forward, preparing to make introductions. He held out a hand towards Mandy.

'I know the young woman already,' George said, giving Mandy an on-off smile. 'Nice to see you having such a nice time, lovey.'

'This is Mr Crabtree, who used to be my boss,' Colin stammered, 'and this is an old colleague, Charlie Winton. Meet a friend of mine, George Packer.'

Crabtree stuck out a hand. 'Nice to meet you, squire.'

George shook Crabtree's hand and Winton's, then turned and stared at Colin again, forcing the initiative on him.

'What'll you have to drink, George?' Crabtree asked.

'Nothing, thanks. I only came to speak to Colin here for a minute. I can't stop.'

'Oh come on now, are you sure?'

'Yes, I'm sure,' George hissed, making it clear he'd be happier if the others cleared off.

'See you in a minute,' Mandy told Colin as she moved off with the frowning Crabtree and the bewildered Winton. From a space at the bar they watched Colin and George. The tension between the pair was as visible as a thong. They were talking, but their mouths scarcely moved. After staring for a minute with his head on one side, Crabtree nudged Mandy and put his mouth close to her ear.

'If I'm not very much mistaken,' he muttered, 'that

young colt in the painted-on trousers is a bit of a pillow-chewer. In fact a damn sight more than a bit of one. What's his business with old Colin?'

Mandy said nothing. Crabtree looked at her. She was gazing down at her drink. Crabtree's frown darkened.

'You don't mean to tell me Colin's in that league as well? Surely to God not . . .'

Mandy looked up at him. 'Does it make him any different from before? He's still Colin, isn't he?'

'I daresay, but . . .' Crabtree looked across the bar again. George had one hand theatrically in the air as he addressed himself to Colin, who looked pale now. 'Bloody hell. I'd never have guessed. Well, well, well . . .'

Colin's pallor was the result of shock. George was telling him, with grim glee, that he would be away from London for six months. He was going to the north to join up with a touring repertory company. Further – if he was to be believed – he was suddenly glad he had taken the decision, which at first had been taken reluctantly.

'I don't know how you can say that, George. How can you be glad? You're telling me we won't set eyes on each other for half a year – '

'Which'll be just long enough for us both to get a sense of proportion – something I reckon we've been sorely in need of. I certainly have, anyway.'

'But things have been so good this past month or so,' Colin protested. 'I thought we'd gotten more settled . . .'

'Oh, things were settling for you, all right. Plenty of work, plenty of money. What about me? Didn't you notice I still had no job? Had you failed to notice I was going steadily out of my head?'

'But I was a consolation to you, you said as much – '

'I'm an actor,' George said. 'I can say any bloody thing and make people believe it. Mind you, you're pretty good in that direction yourself, aren't you?'

'What do you mean?'

'All that shit about being bogged down with work, hardly having a minute to yourself. The weariness, the exhaustion. Then I walk in here and find you living it up. You and the cupcake cutie over there.'

'Hell's bells – that's *Mandy*. She's a mate. She has been for ages. What are you trying to say?'

'I'm saying maybe you should get your head sorted out, that's what I'm saying.'

'George, listen – '

'I've listened long enough, and to enough crap. I'll be seeing you, Sunshine. Have a really great Christmas, won't you?'

At the bar Mandy sighed as she watched George spin on one polished heel and stamp out of the place. She turned away, not wanting to see Colin look so pathetic and lost.

'Listen,' Crabtree said. 'Just tell me something. One thing. Did you know about Colin? When you were working together, I mean?'

'Yes.'

'And it didn't bother you?'

'That's two things you've asked. But no, as it happens, it didn't *bother* me. I don't see why it should bother anybody. There's less harm in Colin Russell than in most men I know.'

'Well . . .' Crabtree swirled his drink. 'Point taken, Mandy. And I'm no flaming bigot, don't go thinking I am. I'm as broad-minded as the next bloke. But bloody hell . . .'

He glanced once at Mandy then downed the remainder of his drink. Charlie Winton, still puzzled, stood gazing across the room at Colin.

* * *

The little club off Ludgate Circus was called Trudi's. Nobody knew why, since no person by the name of Trudi had ever appeared behind the bar or on the tiny cabaret floor, *ever*, and the manager, a fleshy Welshman called Trev, reckoned the real owner was a Greek with a name that was unpronounceable and definitely didn't sound like Trudi.

There was no obvious motif to the place, either in decor or in the type of clientele. Journalists used it, so did photographers, television people, the occasional barrister and a few technicians from a nearby film lab. It was a quiet club, dark-walled, with a long shiny black bar dotted with pools of light from shrouded overhead spotlights. The bar stools were black too, leather-covered with comfortable little backrests and arms. Even the music, when there was any, tended to reflect a preference for quiet about the place; a girl would sit at the baby-grand piano and husk her way through a dozen standards, without once hitting a note that could interrupt the softest conversation.

The only hint of motif came from the fact that the singer was usually the only woman in the place. Women weren't discouraged, they just didn't come. That was because – in Trev's opinion – females didn't go to clubs on their own, and Trudi's cloistered atmosphere did not attract men who were taking the little woman or a girlfriend out for the night. They didn't bring their women because this wasn't a knees-up place, or even a chic after-dinner spot. By some arbitrary evolution, an accident of random events, Trudi's had become an almost men-only place, where conversation and slow drinking were preferred to glitter and revelry.

By midnight there were upwards of thirty customers in the club, more than half of them occupying the bar stools. The singer, a beautiful coloured girl with a diamante clip in her hair, was easing through a neatly diluted version of Lionel Richie's *Hello*. Trev was accepting a drink from a man who looked so tired he should have been in bed.

A few heads turned, looked without much interest and turned away again as a man came in and stood for a moment at the end of the bar. He was in his forties with short-clipped greying hair, restless eyes and a firm, exact mouth. His suit was dark and well-cut, a shade too professional-looking for his surroundings. He ran his gaze along the bar and spotted three vacant stools. Two were near him, the other was close to the far end. He went towards the far one.

'Nobody using this?' he asked.

Colin, hunched in the next seat with a Filofax open on the bar, took a moment to react. He looked up.

'Sorry?'

'Is this stool taken?'

'No. Help yourself.'

Colin closed the book and slipped it in the pocket of his windcheater. He looked at the man again as he sat down. The man returned the glance. There was the unmistakable, universal shimmer of recognition, even though they had never met.

'Bloody cold night,' the man said, rubbing his hands.

'I'll say it is.'

The barman came forward and the man ordered a large scotch. 'And whatever my friend here's having,' he added.

Colin began to refuse, but the man held up his hand.

'A simple friendly gesture,' he said, 'in a sadly friendless world.' He smiled and pointed to Colin's lager glass. 'A pilsner, right?'

'Right. Thanks very much.'

When the barman turned away the man introduced himself as David. Colin identified himself and they shook hands.

'If I may say so, Colin, you look the way I've been feeling for most of the day.'

'And how's that?'

'Cheerless, disconsolate. With me it's my job that did it, and I have to say I've shaken off the gloom by now. You, on the other hand, give me the impression that the condition's only just getting settled in.' David leaned a fraction closer. 'If I'm interfering, just tell me to bugger off.'

'It's all right,' Colin said. 'As it happens I *am* feeling rotten. Personal matters, nothing to do with my job. A bit of civilized conversation would probably help.' He picked up the uncapped bottle the barman had put in front of him and poured half of it into his glass. 'Good health,' he said, raising his drink and sipping at the edge of the froth.

'Good health, indeed,' David said, and swallowed some scotch. 'If there was more of it about I'd be a cheerier chappie.'

'What – health, you mean?'

David nodded. 'I'm a doctor. An immunologist to be precise. Given recent developments, I find my choice of speciality rather ironic.'

Colin nodded, though he didn't know what David was getting at. 'Do you work locally?'

'Sort of. My research work is done in the west of England, but I lecture in London ten days every month. This place was recommended by a colleague as a nice withdrawal spot at the end of the day. I must say I've found the place soothing, the few times I've used it.'

'It's not bad,' Colin agreed. 'I've been coming in at odd times for about two years. It's certainly peaceful.'

David asked what Colin did and he told him.

'Fascinating. I wish, often, that I'd done something artistic, something to protect me from the harsher realities. I sometimes think I'm not cut out for medicine. It requires a man to face up to so much that can scar him. Well *this* man, for one.'

As openers the exchange was good, without strain or artifice. David quickly established his motive: he was out for a quiet drink – stimulating talk was a bonus; he had nothing else in mind. Colin was able, through what he suspected were skilfully planted questions, to make it clear that he was sitting in Trudi's trying to dodge a pain that had been threatening to put him on his knees since early that evening.

Inevitably, on their second drink, David fired an open, probing question: just what, specifically, was getting Colin down? Without any surprise Colin found himself giving a truthful answer – this man was a doctor, after all. It was easier to speak candidly to a doctor. Easier still when the doctor was gay.

'A friend who occasionally likes hurting me has managed to hurt me very badly. I should be used to it, I suppose, but I'm not. I was looking forward to having a good Christmas with my family and with this friend. Now – I suspect – he's made it impossible for me to have anything but a miserable Christmas.'

He explained about George going off to the north, and the manner of his going.

'He's jealous of the girl?' David asked.

'He makes out he is. He does get jealous a lot, even though I try to make him see there's no need. But with Mandy – well, I'm not sure, but I think he used her as a ploy, just a way to make me suffer. Guilt and rejection in one handy package, you know?'

David nodded. He was silent for a minute.

'Colin,' he said finally, 'you really can tell me to mind my own business, I won't be offended. But tell me this if you can. Is he promiscuous, your friend?'

'I don't know.'

'But you can guess, surely.'

Colin toyed with his glass. 'I suspect there are times when he's more promiscuous than anyone I've ever met. But I try never to let that intrude. I think I can make him change, you see.'

'Does "think" really mean "hope against hope"?'

Colin sighed. 'Maybe this conversation wasn't such a good idea.'

'I'm sorry,' David said.

'Don't be. I'm just a bit raw – it's no time to make me face my delusions.'

'No, I suppose not . . .'

'On the other hand, maybe I should. Why do you want to know if he's promiscuous?'

'Because if he is,' David said, his voice tinged with professional gravity, 'I think you should use this period of separation to forget him. Completely. I know it wouldn't be easy, but it would be for the best.' He paused. 'I don't say that simply because the young man is the type who specializes in spiritual torture – although in my opinion that would be reason enough to have done with him. That kind don't change, in my battle-scarred experience.'

Colin sighed at the lights above the bar. 'So what's the other reason for forgetting him?'

David ordered drinks before he went on. He added the contents of his half-finished glass to the fresh one and took a sizable swallow.

'Today,' he said, 'I was called to a ward in the hospital where I teach. There I was shown a patient, a man of twenty-five with an illness diagnosed early this morning as Goodpasture's syndrome. It's a disease that infiltrates the lungs and causes bleeding. It's also very, very rare. Or was, until recently. In America they're seeing more and more cases, practically always among young men. It's a particularly unpleasant disease, Colin. It can lead rapidly to death. At two o'clock today it killed that young man I saw, even though strenuous measures were taken to save his life.'

'That's terrible.'

David nodded. 'Horrible, actually. Horrible because it was another signpost of a kind I've been seeing too often lately. You'll have heard about AIDS, of course.'

'A bit, yes,' Colin said.

'You'll hear a lot more, soon. And a lot of what you'll hear will be hysterical. Already they're using the term "Gay Plague" in the States. A homosexual apartheid has been suggested in some quarters. Even so, prejudiced hysteria or not, it's hard to underplay the disease. Over the pond they have an epidemic and soon there'll be one here, too. The disease, the virus, is spread by people who don't restrict their lovemaking to one partner. Over ninety-percent of people who have it are gay. Hence my remarks about your friend.'

Colin was staring at the bar. 'I thought I felt bad when I came in. Jesus . . .'

'Again, I'm sorry,' David said. 'There's a reforming streak developing in me these days. I can't help going on about this monstrosity. But at the risk of making you feel even worse I have to tell you, Colin, that if we want any hope of survival we're all going to have to change.'

'I read that. And a lot of other things. But it's all so big, so hard to take in. And something in me doesn't want to.'

'Make yourself take it in,' David said, almost harshly.

'I suppose I should, yes . . .'

'This virus leaves its victims helpless in the ruins of their own defences. Think of that, think of the sheer misery. It allows ghastly things to pass unchallenged. And one day, after the sufferer has been clubbed and mutilated by illness after illness, one comes along that kills him.'

David stopped and took a deep breath. He let it out slowly.

'Listen to me going on. But I swear to you, I get bad dreams about this. AIDS is a horrendous blow for our *species*. Probably the worst ever. It's not something you can dare to put from your mind, because it's out to get all of us.' David picked up his glass. 'Now I'll get off the subject. But please don't forget what I've said.'

They talked until past one, then David left. Colin had another drink, although he no longer believed he could drown his misery. He tried, instead, to contain it without weeping.

4

Christmas Eve was a Monday. Ena Russell got up early and after a swift breakfast prepared by Colin – sugar-free cereal, tea, toast – she got out the polish and a handful of dusters and started on the seasonal jobs she insisted on doing, even though Colin complained they should be left to him.

'It'll be a black day,' Ena argued, 'when I can't polish and dust my own living room and my ornaments and put out clean sideboard covers and such. It's a job that needs a woman's special touch at Christmas, anyhow.'

Her special touch had been losing its edge since the onset of her cataracts. Her bouts of absent-mindedness contributed their share to the appearance of well-shone disorder she tended to leave behind her. Last Christmas Colin had spent half an hour putting things back in place and finishing little jobs Ena had left half-done. He'd even had to get out the dust pan and sweep up the pine needles Ena had dislodged from the tree every time she bumped its branches – which had been often.

Today Colin worked upstairs in his studio, pausing every few minutes to listen to his mother hum and mutter away around the living room. For as long as he could remember, her mouth-music and monologues had been a background to anything he did at home – his homework as a boy, his leisure reading, his hours at the drawing board sharpening his skills.

There had been another voice, too, one he missed badly. It was the voice that used to render booming impersonations of Elvis Presley and Roy Orbison, the extrovert voice that cracked gags, laughed a lot and never failed to shape the atmosphere to its mood. Bill's voice. And today Colin was getting his work done early, because big brother Bill was coming to visit.

The job on hand had begun as a straightforward commission – a package design for a low-fat cheese product. There was no question of having to break new ground; trends in that kind of design had been established; it was simply a matter of coming up with an idea that would fall within the currently accepted boundaries. Colin knew exactly how to proceed on the job. First he did his homework on packaged dairy goods – market research results, product analysis, export design considerations and advertising feedback on food items similar to the one he was handling. He produced three draft designs and submitted them to the client. The client said no, they weren't really what he had in mind.

Colin tried again. This time he took the trends to the limit. His designs broke some of the current rules, but stuck to enough of them to look dynamic without being outlandish.

The client was impressed. But he said no again.

Colin was stumped. He went back to his homework. He studied cheese and butter packaging design over a ten-year period, checked dozens of successful designs for their persuasive elements, read up on what the pundits said about visually selling health-orientated products to an additive-suspicious public. All he learned was that his designs were as on-the-ball as he could make them.

So he told the client that. The client said well, he could see the designs were good – very good, come to that. But something was missing, he felt. Would Colin consider having another go, because the client really felt he was the man for the job.

A sleepless night followed. In the morning – the Friday

before Christmas – Colin rolled out of bed, empty of energy or ideas and glumly resigned to telling the client the deal was off. Then, as he waited for the kettle to boil, a small thought struck.

He hadn't done a retrospective analysis of the client's package designs. All he had done was check the trends and fall in line with them. So Colin went down to the supermarket and did some research. Ten minutes into the project he felt like kicking himself. The client's designs were modern, all right. They sold the goods. But they broke one rule that Colin had always stood by. Hurrying back home he recalled a lecturer laying that rule on him over and over: *Visual form must realize a stated task; a pretty picture doesn't serve a commercial purpose simply by having a line of type stuck above or below it.*

Except that was the way Colin's client sold his stuff. He used modern typography and stylish illustration – but the illustrations had practically nothing to do with the words they accompanied – and the words never crossed into the territory of the pictures, as they did in Colin's layouts.

In four hours he produced three new designs. Within another hour he was speeding eastward to Kensington with them. The client almost cried with pleasure at what he saw.

So now, early on Christmas Eve, Colin was pushing hard to finish the final, full-scale, camera-ready artwork. He had won himself solid future contracts on the basis of this one, and he had picked up a priceless piece of wisdom along the way: rules are dispensable, even the precious ones.

At ten o'clock he stopped and went downstairs to check on Ena. She was still pottering in the living room, working in a lemon-scented haze as she squirted polish at every surface that might benefit from a coat.

'Time for a tea-break, Mum.'

'I've only a couple of bits to do and I'm finished.'

Colin looked round the room. There was a green patch of needles on the carpet again. Polish had been sprayed on the coffee table and left to dry to a grey film. Somehow, two strings of tinsel had been dislodged from the picture rail and were hanging down on the mantelpiece.

'You've done enough for now,' he said. 'Put down your aerosol and come and have a sit.'

Ena shuffled into the kitchen while Colin was filling the kettle.

'The place'll never be ready for our Bill coming if I don't get on with it,' she complained.

'Twelve o'clock he said he'd be here, right?' Colin plugged in the kettle and switched it on. 'You've bags of time.'

'I've got to get myself ready as well, though. Don't forget that.'

'Mum – stop worrying. You've all the time you need. As soon as you've finished in the living room I'll get out the Hoover and have a quick belt round the house with it. You can take yourself off to your room and tittivate to your heart's content.'

'Well, if you say so . . .'

Ena eased herself down on a chair. Colin glanced at her, noticing how tired she looked. In the space of eight or nine months she had begun to age alarmingly. Colin felt a sharp, fleeting pang of sadness; Mum was getting old, and what had been would never be again.

'I'm really looking forward to seeing my big silly son.' Ena laughed softly. 'He was always the joker, wasn't he?'

'Life and soul,' Colin said, setting out two cups and saucers. He looked forward to seeing his brother as much as Ena did. It had been summer when they last met. 'What have you got him for Christmas, by the way?'

'A shirt. He always said he could never have enough shirts.'

'I've got him an electronic notebook. That'll give him the edge on his mates, all right.'

'And what's an electric notebook when it's at home?'

'Elec*tronic*. It's a little tape recorder for speaking your notes into, instead of having to write them down.'

Ena tutted. 'Sounds a bit pricey. You shouldn't be throwing your money about. Especially not now.'

Colin smiled to himself. The stigma of his self-employment had been erased by a flattering piece in the local paper, headed by a picture of Colin at his drawing board. He had engineered the coverage through an old pal who was deputy editor on the paper, and it had served its purpose admirably. Ena bought ten copies of the paper and sent the article to as many relatives as she could think of. She walked the length of the street with visibly expanded pride these days, too. Her son was a real businessman with a business of his own – the paper said so. But in her heart Ena still couldn't believe that Colin was better off now he was freelancing. A man with no boss was a man with no proper job, and no proper job meant no proper wage coming in. That was an indelible law and Colin saw no point in wasting his energy trying to make his mother believe otherwise.

'It's such a pity Bill can't stop,' Ena said. 'He hasn't spent Christmas with us since that first year after he moved away. I sometimes think she deliberately finds ways to keep him from coming here.'

'Be fair, Mum.' Colin was rotating the teapot, speeding the infusion. 'Eunice – or *She*, as you keep calling her, has got a tough life with three young kids to look after and Bill away from home as often as he is. I mean they're a separate family, aren't they? They'll want to spend Christmas on their own. It's only natural.'

'Mm.' Ena folded her hands huffily. 'A man's mother has a right to see him, whether he's married or not.'

Colin poured the tea, wondering how it would have been if he'd moved away, too. He could have, more than once. There was a time he almost did, then found he couldn't bear the thought of his mother being on her own. A relationship had perished because he'd decided not to leave, but he hardly regretted that.

'I suppose you'll be hogging him for a while, down at that smelly old pub.'

'I'd have a job keeping him out of it,' Colin said. 'That's one of the things he misses most – the Paxton. He learned his drinking in there, Mum. The place reeks with nostalgia for Bill.'

'He taught you your boozing there, too, didn't he?' Ena's tone was the one she should have forgotten when Bill and Colin grew up, but she had chosen to hang on to it. When she spoke that way she was addressing a wayward boy. 'I remember the night he brought you in, that very first time. You could hardly walk. And still you went back. Drinkers never learn sense.'

Colin put his mother's tea in front of her.

'Two pints of draught cider,' he said. 'That's what did it. I still feel queasy when I smell the stuff.'

Thoughts of happy days danced as he got his own tea and sat down opposite his mother. The practical jokes, the bike-chases round the streets, the old gang, the laughter. The essence of it all had been laughter, a kind Colin had never known since. He believed it had finally gone out of his life when his brother did.

'Have you finished your work?' Ena asked.

'Just a bit to do. Not much.'

'Well see you finish it, won't you? With nobody pushing you, there's always the temptation to let things slip.'

'The client's pushing me,' Colin said. 'My hunger for vast riches is pushing me. Don't panic.'

When they had finished their tea Colin went back to his studio and promised himself he wouldn't step outside that door until the layout was finished. Since he knew he had to be out of the room again soon the incentive to concentrate was strong. But perversely, concentration began to falter. He made three mistakes in less than a minute and sat back, wondering what was up.

It was thinking and talking about Bill that had done it, he supposed. More precisely, it had been the memories of the old days, invading the present and forcing him to understand what was lost. Christmas was a time for that, as much as for anything else.

It had been as normal and happy a boyhood as any lad could have wanted. But it had been more than that. Colin chewed his pencil, wondering at the strong, nameless undercurrent those times had carried. He was more aware of it every time he cast his mind back.

And now, suddenly, he realized what it had been. His boyhood had been overseen, supervised, managed and protected by the finest friend he'd ever had – Bill Russell, his brother.

He had never thought of Bill as his best friend before. But that was what he'd been. Colin had looked up to no one more, had felt safer with no one, had never drawn such warmth and happiness from a living soul as he had from his brother.

God how he'd loved that brother of his!

And still did, he reminded himself, though it wasn't the same as before. That fierce current had been unique. It had been a compound of things, powerful things – natural brotherly affection, plus the re-directed love for a father Colin had scarcely known, plus solid-gold hero worship for a bloke who could make ten of any other kind.

Realizing that, feeling its echo, Colin understood something else. All these years later he was still overshadowed by his early devotion to Bill. The hero-worship had cooled with the saner perspectives of adulthood, and so had the other elements of his adoration. But that stature of Bill's was still there, even if it was only a phantom. It held power over Colin. *Still.*

It was a shock to realize that his life, without that formidable shadow, might have been wildly different. Might even have worked out better. But what a grand, admirable shadow to live in, all the same.

Colin looked at his watch, sighed and leaned over the board again. As he willed himself to concentrate he smiled, realizing one more thing. He was probably a bit of a mother's boy, as a lot of people believed. But he was even more of a big-brother's boy.

By three o'clock the excitement had proved too much for Ena. Sitting in her regally stuffed chair by the fire with her older son opposite and Colin stretched out on the sofa, she drifted into a post-lunch slumber while Bill was talking about the trouble they'd had getting an extension built on their house in Devon.

'She's off,' Colin said, nodding towards his mother.

Bill smiled, but it was a troubled smile. He shifted his feet and sat back in his chair, as if someone had just left the room and he could relax more.

'She's changed a lot, Colin. A hell of a lot. Not just her appearance, either. She's aged in all kinds of ways.'

'Nobody gets younger.'

'You know what I mean,' Bill said. 'Mum's got older than her years. And it's happened so fast. Makes you wonder what she'll be like in another year.'

Colin nodded, not wishing to say anything about his own tentative fears. Apart from the signs Bill had noticed, there were brief periods when Ena behaved as if she were sliding into senile decay. The doctor had explained that sudden changes in her sugar levels caused it to happen. That was small comfort. What Colin saw at those times was a frightening glimpse of the future, when his mother's personality would wither and she would be nothing but a replica of herself, without wit or reason.

'You've got older yourself,' Colin said, grinning, forcing the talk on to a less serious level. 'Touch of grey at the temples, neat little weary lines under the eyes. It gives you a sort of distinguished look.'

'Eunice is kind about it, too,' Bill said. 'She tells me I look like a young David Jacobs. Smart, huh? Never tell anybody who they're looking older than.'

'How do you think I'm holding up?'

Bill tilted his head a fraction. 'Hmm. You look the same as last time. Thinner, maybe, but self-employment does that to people. On the outside I'd say you look fine. In the pub, though, I got the impression the inner man's the one in need of refurbishing.'

Colin was surprised. They had been out for less than an hour, and during that time they talked about nothing but their work, with the odd diversion into nostalgia when old faces were seen in the crowd.

'What makes you think that? Something I said?'

'No.' Bill clasped his hands and leaned forward, the way he had always done when he confided anything. There was authority in the movement, and confidence; Colin felt he knew he was still talking to the one who lived in his shadow. 'You're jumpy, Colin. You used to be placid. Now you fiddle with things when you talk and you do it even more when you listen. You've developed one or two twitchy head movements, too. You're too uptight.'

'Self-employment again,' Colin said, trying to smile off Bill's remarks. 'It makes a fella tense.'

'It's more than that.' A re-clasping of the hands, then Bill hit home, as he could always do. 'How's your private life?'

Colin tensed with the effort of trying to look casual. He waved his hand, taking in the living room, the house, 'This is my private life.'

Bill sighed. 'You're a glib swine, Colin. You defuse questions you don't want to answer, and that makes it seem as if you've answered them. And I suppose it works with most people. *Most* people. But since you're my brother I won't push the fact that you're keeping something from me. I'd hate to think you're suffering some misery in silence, though.'

'Don't worry about me. I'm fine.'

Bill's assessments could be uncomfortable. Once, two or three years before, he had called Colin a chameleon. He explained the remark by pointing out that whatever company Colin found himself in, he could make himself blend. Even his accent changed, Bill said, to suit the ones around him. He could be near-cockney or decidedly Hampstead, depending on the circumstances.

'Is it enough for you?' Bill asked, after looking at his sleeping mother for a moment.

'What?'

'This. The life you have. I think about you often and I wonder if you're a lonely man.'

'My work absorbs me, Bill. Looking after Mum's quite a distraction, too. I don't have time to pine for a kind of life I don't have. And I do have a lot of freedom other men my age don't have.'

'Practically the fulfilled man,' Bill said, nodding.

'Well . . .'

'That's what I wanted to be.' Bill drew his hand slowly

over his face, and the effect was like a conjuring trick. A mask had dropped away. He looked stark, suddenly, his features open and vulnerable. 'I thought I had the formula all worked out, too. It was the usual formula, nothing original – financial security, a loyal wife, fine kids, a good home. I've got all that and enough insurances, one way and another, to make sure I *keep* it all. But I don't feel fulfilled.'

Colin was surprised. 'What do you feel?'

'Fed up, most of the time. Occasionally I even feel cheated.'

This was not a welcome development. Heroes' feet should be shrouded in mist, so that their composition is unknown; father-figures' home truths ought to be kept to themselves; protectors' failed dreams are their own business, never to be disseminated. Colin did not want to know that Bill, of all people, was less than square with the world. Stiffening against what he had just heard, he received another blow.

'I told you, I think about you a lot,' Bill said, his voice too candid for comfort. 'I'll tell you why. I envy you. I've spent years envying you.'

Colin sat up and planted his feet on the floor. 'Me? How can the likes of you envy the likes of *me*?'

'That freedom you were on about. The option to be footloose. That's cause enough . . .'

'Aw come off it, Bill – '

'There's a dozen reasons. I asked you if you're lonely – I asked that out of hope, I suppose. Maybe you weren't to be envied after all. But of course you are. Even with whatever it is that's biting you, you're miles better off than I am. Than I'll ever be.'

'The beer down the Paxton's too strong for you nowadays,' Colin said, clutching at a passing straw. 'It's made you maudlin. You're set up, for God's sake. You're a success.'

'I'm a salesman of burglar alarm systems,' Bill said. 'I'm a husband who performs a husband's duties from habit. I'm a clockwork father without one shred of anything . . . What's the word . . . *spontaneous* in the way I behave towards my kids. And I can hold my beer, Colin. If anything's making me open up to you, it's a long-standing need to do it. Christmas brings things out of people.'

'I'll say it does,' Colin murmured, rubbing his forehead.

'Sorry,' Bill said. 'It's just – oh, I walked through that door today and saw the two of you and I remembered. It was like a flood of heartache. This was the centre of everything, once. What keeps the heat under my regret is that you're still here and you're still part of it. The good old back-then life. The life with options.'

'Bill – will you talk about something else?' Colin stood up. 'I'm not good at having the carpet whipped out from under. All these years I've been . . .' He clamped his mouth tight and shook his head. 'Never mind. Let's just get on to something else.'

'Christ,' Bill groaned, 'I didn't mean to upset you like this . . .'

Ena stirred in her chair and her eyes opened slowly. She looked at Colin, then at Bill, her face blank.

'You nodded off,' Bill said, the cheerful mask instantly restored.

'Lord almighty.' Ena clapped a hand over her mouth and yawned. 'How long was I out?'

'Only a couple of minutes,' Colin said. 'I think this is a perfect time for me to make coffee. Sit tight, the pair of you. If you're quiet and don't squabble, you can have After Eights on your saucers.'

He was halfway to the kitchen when the telephone rang.

'I'll get it. Probably my low-fat cheese client checking up to make sure I'm still sweating over his design.'

He went into the hall and snatched up the receiver. 'Hello?' The line crackled. 'Colin Russell here. Hello?'

'Hi,' a distant voice said. 'It's George.'

Colin's breath caught. 'Ah . . .' He coughed. 'Hello. This is a surprise.'

'I'm calling to wish you Merry Christmas.'

'Merry Christmas to you.'

'Didn't send you a card. They cost the same as a burger nowadays. I'm bumming this phone, so I'll make it quick – '

'How have things been?'

'Rough. But pretty enjoyable, I suppose.' There was a pause with muttering in the background. Colin got the feeling somebody was annoyed. After a couple of seconds George came back. 'Hey, Col, you still there?'

'Yeah, I'm here.'

'Just have a nice Christmas. I've got to split. I'll be thinking about you.'

The line died. Colin put the receiver down slowly.

'Who was it?' Ena called.

'A friend. Calling to wish me a happy Christmas.'

He put his hands over his eyes. The season of sincerity and soul-baring and changes of heart was getting way too much for him. He took a deep breath to steady himself and went through to the kitchen.

'Why?' he hissed as he spooned coffee into the filter.

He glanced at the door, hoping no one had heard. He hadn't meant to make a sound, although the question filled his head so fiercely it was no wonder it leaked out.

Why, why, why?

He had been starting to cope. The few dreams and

dependancies left to him had been rearranged and they had become an adequate support. Until today. Now the props had been kicked away.

Why do people do it?

He wanted to forget what Bill had told him, and he had been beginning to forget George ever existed. He picked up the coffee jug and stared at it. Either I'm too good for this world, he thought, or I'm catching it in the teeth for something terrible I've done.

5

In the third week of January Colin was contacted by the Milestone Agency in the Gray's Inn Road. The female caller said their Graphic Projects Manager wanted to discuss a new design contract. She wouldn't be more specific than that. If he was interested, she said, he should be at the Milestone offices for two-thirty the following day.

Colin had no previous dealings with the agency. He checked their track record and discovered, alarmingly, that they handled some of the biggest airline and department-store promotional accounts in the country. He decided to wear a tie.

Milestone's Graphic Projects Manager, Mr Lamont, was a tall, stooping man in his late fifties. Bushy-eyebrowed, hook-nosed and dressed roughly twenty years behind the times, he was the kind of man Colin would have expected to find at a corner desk in an accounts department.

Until he spoke.

'Come in, sit down and be impressed,' he said, pointing to a steel and leather chair in front of his desk. 'This office was designed to underline one of our most firmly held company views – good taste doesn't matter a shit if you've got money to fling around.'

Colin trod the white wool carpet gingerly, convinced he'd make marks on it. As he sat down he looked around him. The walls of the place were covered in big silver picture frames, maybe twenty of them, displaying prize-winning examples of Milestone promotional work – four-colour magazine ads, showcards, package designs and company logos. Mr Lamont's desk – two-inch thick plate glass on sturdy teak plinths – was backed by a floor-to-ceiling, wall-to-wall window with a rainbow-hued venetian blind, half-open to art-direct the daylight. To one side of the desk was a tall cabinet displaying gold, silver and bronze awards in a variety of shapes. Against the opposite wall was a long, low sideboard with a pale blue top and white enamelled doors; on top was a gleaming chrome expresso machine and a set of gold plated optic stands holding bottles of whisky, gin, brandy, vermouth and rum. Mixers and glasses were grouped on a silver gallery tray alongside.

'Wow', Colin said.

Lamont sat down and clasped his hands on the desk. 'I don't know if you're aware of it or not,' he said, 'but the patron saint of advertising is Bernadine of Siena.'

'I hadn't heard,' Colin admitted.

'Nor had I, until the directors told me they wanted to put a life-size sculpture of her in the corner there. I managed to persuade them it was a bit over the top, even by Milestone's standards. So instead, they're giving me a designer hat stand, for sweet Jesus' sake.' Lamont sat back. 'So you're the man who designed the Clifton-Treece centenary shield.'

Colin had to think for a moment. 'Oh. Yes, I did that.'

'You'd nearly forgotten it.'

Colin nodded.

'Well, the qualities of draughtsmanship and shall we say, uh, company-image-aptness, were what attracted our attention to your work. I know it was only a minor project for you, but it's often the small jobs that say the nicest things behind your back.'

Lamont put one hand on the back of his head, the other on the desk. It was one of those authoritarian moves Bill could make, a simple re-arranging of the self that commanded undivided attention.

'We want you to consider a design project which, in itself, is only a part of a broader contract we've been awarded by Brauhaus AG, who are broadening their UK operation with uncanny speed.'

Colin had been reading about them in the newspapers and trade press. Brauhaus were a motor parts chain store based in Munich. They already had eight megastores and fifty or more high street branches in Britain, selling everything from car dusters and petrol caps to electronic tuning gear and heavy workshop tackle.

'You're not the only graphic designer we're putting on the project,' Lamont continued. 'There are others, and I'd say they're in the same league as you. So you see, I'm not offering you a job. I'm giving you the chance to compete for one. Are you interested?'

'What's the project?'

'We want a design for a credit card.'

Colin frowned. 'I've done credit cards before . . .'

'We've seen them,' Lamont said. 'But I say again, it was the centenary shield that got us interested in your work. You see, this credit card will be held by very few people. It'll be a prestige item the customer will be happy to let fall accidentally on the table over dinner – like the gold Visa or the platinum Amex. So someone with a flair for the heraldic style is more likely to land the commission than some wallah who's just good at designing cards.'

'What's the deal, exactly?' Colin asked. He was hooked on the notion already, but there was no sense acting too keen.

'Whatever designer we settle on – and I'll point out here that the decision will be solely ours, since Brauhaus don't want to be concerned with such trifles – that designer will be expected to make a number of alterations and refinements to the design until we and Brauhaus are jointly happy that the layout is precisely right for the job. So – we're talking about monopolising a month of your time, should you be successful in landing the commission.'

Lamont paused, waiting for Colin to say something. Something about money, Colin guessed. In which case he would keep his mouth shut, since he knew one or two agency adages about people who were more interested in the price than the job.

'We have more than a rough idea of your fees, Mr Russell.' Another pause, this one for effect. 'We would triple your typical charge for a project of this kind – and, of course, the retainer fee would be over and above, at our usual rates.'

Colin nodded, knowing that if he spoke at this point his voice would be at the squeaky end of its register.

'Now naturally,' Lamont said, 'I'm not asking you to go away and turn out some designs that might not earn you a penny if they're rejected. You'll be paid for your initial work, usual illustrators' rates, whether it's accepted or not. How does all that grab you?'

'It's a generous offer,' Colin said, feeling that it was safest to state the obvious.

'We're generous people.' Lamont took a manila envelope from a neat stack at the end of the desk. He slid it towards Colin. 'That's the Brauhaus bumff pack. Marketing policy, design samples, customer targeting, the usual stuff. Absorb it and let me have your submissions as soon as you can.'

Colin took the envelope. 'How many other designers are trying for the job?'

'That,' Lamont said, 'is for us to know and for you to wonder about.' He nodded at the stack of envelopes. 'There could be a clue there. But remember, you don't know how many people I've seen before you.' He stood and extended his hand. 'Best of luck, Mr Russell.'

Colin shook his hand firmly. 'I'll be in touch, Mr Lamont. Thanks very much.'

That evening, as an aid to concentration, Colin took his preliminary notes to the Paxton and settled himself at a corner table with a pint. Already he'd covered four pages with observations gleaned from the information pack and articles about Brauhaus AG in trade magazines. He also had sketches of ten recent credit cards that had been nominated for design awards. His task now was to marry a composite of design ideas to the company's image – and to the elitist angle of the commission.

It would be no easy job. A few years before it would have been easier. Now, dozens of companies were issuing credit cards. New ones appeared practically every week. It was getting harder to be original, harder still to come up with a layout that would stand out from the others.

Ordinarily the Paxton was the ideal place for Colin to generate ideas. The buzz of conversation, the soothingly beer-and-tobacco scented atmosphere, the soft, warm lighting, the downright familiarity – that was a formula for inspiration as strong as any Colin knew. But tonight there was a problem. It came in the shape – or shapelessness – of Andy Riordan. He was a man Colin had known since boyhood, a rough-hewn cockney-Irish market trader who had been born to his calling. Andy was permanently in need of a shave, it seemed, and his clothes had an excessively lived-in look. He was overweight and always sweated heavily, even in the cold weather. If he had one outstanding feature, though, it was his friendliness. Andy was friendly to the point of overkill.

He was on his third pint when he spotted Colin, sitting alone at the corner table, bowed over his notes. Andy launched himself away from the bar and fired out a greeting to herald his approach.

'Oi then, Colin! How's it goin', mate?'

Colin knew who it was without looking up. He sighed softly.

'Haven't seen you in yonks.' Andy pulled out a chair and sat down. 'I read the bit in the local rag. Things are lookin' up, eh?'

'Yeah, they could be worse.' Colin looked down wistfully at his notes. So much for peace. So much for inspiration. 'How's tricks, Andy?'

'Still earnin' a crust. I've had to change my lines around a bit, though.'

'What are you flogging now?'

'Hi-tech novelty lines. Every bugger's novelty-mad these days.' Andy drew his cuff across his shiny forehead. 'Everythin's got to be electronic too, or it's piggin' useless. I'll tell you somethin', I've got lines that had to be invented just to use up spare chunks of circuit that didn't have a use.' He sniffed disdainfully. 'I can do you a really necessary currency converter that you wear round your neck. Dead essential, that. Or a car burglar alarm that does more than let out a blast of noise if anybody as much as looks at your motor – it purifies the air, checks the outside temperature and tells you the time. Or how about this one – just the thing for a man like yourself, Col. A bookmark that bleeps to tell you where you've left your favourite book. All you have to do is whistle. Now it's time you had somethin' like that, intit? I mean, how have you got along without one?'

'Things like that are spin-offs,' Colin said. 'The real technology at the heart of it all is useful, in most cases.' He always defended gadgetry, since he was particularly addicted to it. 'I don't know what I'd do without my computer.'

'People managed without them before,' Andy pointed out.

'But not so well. Without the computer, it'd take me a lot more time to get my designs together. Some of them, anyway. And look at the storage – instead of cramming drawers with piles of paper I can keep it electronically, mountains of it, tucked away in one tiny corner of the drawer.'

Andy sat back, looking thoughtful. 'You mean the computer designs your stuff? Isn't that a bit – well, dishonest? No offence, but I'd have thought you'd too much pride to stand aside while a flamin' machine did your work for you.'

Colin smiled. 'The machine is a servant, Andy. A willing one, and very fast. It can't do anything by itself, it has to be told. I tell it, I create my design using its facilities, then I instruct it to give me a high-speed printout. I work from that.'

'Sold,' Andy said, grinning. 'I'll have three, guv.' He pointed at the notebook on the table. 'What're you workin' on now?'

'A credit card.'

Andy craned his neck, looking at the sketches. 'Fascinatin' things, ain't they? I mean, you spend money without transferrin' anythin' at all out of your pocket into the till. That's got to cut down the old sales resistance, intit?'

'I'll say. You go out with a credit card, you come home with it still in your pocket. But in the meantime you could've spent a hundred quid, or more.'

Andy nodded. 'I wish I could take credit cards, I'll tell you that. The wife's got one an' it's like a knife through me bank account.' Andy squinted at the drawings again. 'What's it goin' to look like, then?'

'That's the problem,' Colin said. 'It's got to look very special. It has to be distinctive, and its image has to register pretty fast, too. It's got a lot of competition to overcome – and I suspect I have, too.'

Andy puckered his lips, looking thoughtful again. 'Money,' he said. 'It ought to look like money.'

'How do you make that out?'

'Well for one thing, money's got a right distinguished look about it, right? Banknotes have got class.'

Colin nodded, warming to Andy's secret wisdom.

'Right. So like you said, Col, you don't part with a credit card, even though you're spendin' like there's no tomorrow. So think how much more attractive the thing is if you get to keep it, an' it *looks* like it's worth a bomb. Its looks remind you what kind of power it's got. People would queue up for one like that, I reckon.'

Colin thought immediately of American Express. That one was particularly powerful in design – and it resembled money. There was a figurehead on it. He was starting to get excited.

'Andy, I think you're on to something.' Colin scribbled a note in his book and slapped it shut. 'Drink up. I'm buying.'

An hour later he was back at his drawing board. Every few seconds his pencil made stabbing forays across a big sheet of cartridge paper as he scanned through a fat book called *Banknote Design*.

It was amazing. Money did have that special aura. Colin copied down details of Italian, German and Spanish currency, noting features they all had in common and highlighting aspects that distinguished this or that note from the others. The more he studied the glossy reproductions the more fascinated he became. Here was nothing less than the dignity and power of great paintings and lofty frescoes. Money's image had precisely the clout the Brauhaus card needed. Andy Riordan had got it right. Colin had never been so glad to be interrupted in his life.

By ten o'clock two clear designs were emerging. Each, in its way, had the serious and opulent look of money, without emulating a banknote too closely. Colin was standing back from his pair of preliminary sketches when he heard a bump downstairs.

He turned, puzzled, listening. There was no further sound. He looked at the clock. It was his mother's bedtime. Round about now she would have looked in on him to say goodnight. Anxious suddenly, Colin went out on to the landing. Still no sound. He took the stairs two at a time and found his mother lying in the kitchen, an overturned chair beside her.

'Mum?'

On his knees he touched her face, felt the feeble pulse at her neck. She was terrifyingly pale. Colin went out to the hall and grabbed the telephone.

Ena was in hospital within fifteen minutes. Colin was given a chair and a cup of tea and told not to worry. It was five minutes to midnight before he could really stop worrying, though. That was when an incredibly young looking doctor came and made explanations.

He told Colin that his mother had suffered an attack of hypoglycaemia. The level of sugar in her blood had dropped and she had gone into a coma.

'We've given her glucose intravenously and she's come round now.'

'Can I see her?'

'Sure,' the doctor said. 'But you'll have to keep it brief. She's very tired.'

Ena was in a very white-looking bed, wearing her best pink nightie which Colin had put in a carrier bag when the ambulance arrived. She didn't seem as pale as before, but her lips were blue and she had difficulty keeping her eyes open.

'I don't know what happened,' she told Colin.

'It was a little turn, Mum. Nothing for you to worry about. They'll have you sorted out in a couple of days.'

'That hypo-whatsit thing again, was it?'

Colin nodded. 'They're giving you glucose through that tube.'

'The needle doesn't hurt, funnily enough.' Ena sighed and raised a hand, then let it flop back on the bed. 'I've hardly the strength to move myself,' she said. 'Are they sure I'm going to be all right?'

'Positive.'

'Will you let Bill know? He should know, I think.'

'I'll give him a ring. But you'll be out of hospital soon and you can talk to him yourself.'

'I thought maybe he'd come and see me.'

'He will, if he can. You've got to remember he's out on the road a lot. I might only be able to speak to Eunice and she'll have to pass on a message. By the time Bill gets it you might be back home.'

Colin watched Ena take that in. He was sure she was beginning to lose her handhold on life. This had been the first coma. What would be next? It was nearly impossible now to see the woman she had been when he was young. She was old, and illness was hastening her towards something more than old, something worse.

'I want to sleep, Colin.' Her eyes were already closed. 'Come and see me tomorrow, won't you.'

He promised he would.

Ena mumbled something else, but she was too close to sleep for it to carry on the air. Colin leaned forward and kissed her cheek.

'Night night, Mum.'

When he got home he stood in the silent hallway, knowing he wouldn't be able to sleep. He wasn't sure if he could work, either. He made coffee, filled a flask with it and took it to his room.

The drawings looked different now. His enthusiasm had dropped away and he saw the work with a much colder eye. If one thing stood out, it was the over-elaboration. The drawings looked as if they'd been made by a Victorian artist. There were curlicues and rosettes where there should have been clean lines and open spaces. Brevity and economy were virtues of contemporary art; they were nowhere evident in those preliminary drawings. Colin studied them for ten minutes, then tore them up.

Beginning again was agony. He couldn't get his mother out of his mind. He kept wondering what might have happened if she'd collapsed while she was working at the cooker. Or if she had been holding a hot drink. Or using a knife.

'Stop it, for God's sake!'

The pointless speculation faded, but he was still dominated by the image of Ena lying in that bed, looking so old and sick. Colin sighed and began to sense the spectre of failure hovering over this project. How could he put his heart into it now? And he wasn't deluded – it needed all of his enthusiasm, and his capacity for self-criticism. How could he possibly . . .

This is defeatism, he told himself sharply. He was a professional, he was supposed to function under any amount of stress. Loss of heart was out. He poured himself a cup of coffee and drank down half of it, even though it scalded his throat. With fresh paper on the board and a tub of sharp pencils at his side he set to making a reality of the theme he knew would work, if he threw all of himself into it.

After half a dozen false starts, a keen stylishness began to show. Colin worked in bursts, stopping every few minutes to refresh his eye, flipping through the banknote book and making mental adaptations of existing designs. As he worked on one design other ideas emerged and he copied them down in rough form at the edge of the paper, to be enlarged upon later.

By two o'clock he had one detailed first draft and was halfway through another. They were better this time. Much better. The layouts still had the unmistakable quality of money, but they had a lot more flair now. Colin stopped for another cup of coffee. While he was pouring it the telephone beside him rang, tearing the room's silence. He jumped, almost spilling the coffee, then stared as the 'phone rang again. Something was wrong. The hospital were getting ready to deliver bad news. Trembling, scared, Colin put down the flask and cup. His hand hovered over the receiver, then he snatched it up.

'Colin Russell,' he said, dry-mouthed.

'Now there's a voice it's good to hear.'

Colin took a deep breath. It was George.

'It's me, Col. George.'

'Yeah, I know. Do you realize what time it is?'

'Well, I know it's late. Or early, depending on how you look at it. I'm at a party, and you know how time goes haywire when you're living it up. I've been meaning to call you for a couple of weeks now. How are things? Still the big success, are you?'

'I'm getting by.'

'You sound kind of down.'

'I am. My mother was taken ill a few hours ago. She's in hospital. I was trying to force myself through some work and get her off my mind.'

'Is she going to be all right?'

'Yes, I think so. Or I hope so.'

'Oh, dear.' George was silent for a couple of seconds. Colin heard people laughing in the background. He was wishing, earnestly, that this call had never been made. 'Well,' George said, 'let's hope it all works out.'

'Yeah, let's hope,' Colin said. 'How are you getting along?'

'Pretty well. We went down a bomb in Bolton last

week. Next week we're playing in Manchester. The way I look at it, this may not exactly be the kind of acting or the type of company I'd see myself staying with, but it's like piano practice, right? I'm not taking my skills any further forward, but I'm keeping in shape.'

'Glad it's working out,' Colin said flatly. He was beginning to feel bad again. George was too disturbing; even his voice carried the threat of unsettled days. 'I hope this stint leads to bigger things for you.'

'Thanks. Listen, Colin, there's something I wanted to ask you. How would you like to come on a visit? When we're doing Manchester, say? It'd be a real treat to see you.'

This was the man who could treat him like dirt, Colin thought. The man who could make him squirm with embarrassment and pain – the man who had put him through more misery, perhaps, than anyone else before.

'I'd like to come up, George. But my work's got to take priority. I've got a heavy job on, and what with that, and Mum being ill, I'm just not going to have any free time.'

There was a long pause, then George spoke again, his voice colder now. He said he understood.

'You know how the pressures can build up,' Colin said, hating to sound as if he was handing out a rejection, even though he was. 'I mean it's the middle of the night and here I am, working . . .'

'I understand perfectly,' George said, sounding petulant. 'Look, I'll have to buzz. There's a tiny piece of action I'd like to get in on. See you around, Colin.'

'Listen, George – '

''Bye.'

There was a click and the line began to hum. Colin put down the receiver and picked up his coffee. If he had been unsettled before, this was worse. This, he believed, was something he couldn't fight his way through.

The precise name for what he felt was heartache. It could crush him. At that moment, growing tired, aching in spirit, he knew he could do no more work. He would have to sleep, and in the morning he would have to wake and wait for it all to seep back to him, all the worry and the edging despair and the hurt.

If only George hadn't called. If only Colin could be sure he never would again. Things had to heal, for God's sake. How could healing take place when the wound kept opening again? If he'd more common sense, he'd just tell George it was all over between them, period. But common sense didn't stand a chance, Colin suspected.

He stared at his drawings, smothering a yawn. There lay his only solace, he thought. His work was his salvation, and it was the only major thing in his life that didn't hurt him.

6

Mr Lamont was leaning on the edge of his desk, the palms of his hands propping him on either side. The illusion was unsettling; the glass top would obviously have been bevelled and made safe, but to Colin it looked as if Lamont was poised on a razor's edge, and one wrong move would slice his hands in half.

'I suppose you're wondering why I asked you to come here,' Lamont said, ' – to quote the classic dynamic chairman's opening statement. Sit down. I've something to tell you.'

Colin lowered himself into the leather and chrome, wishing he could fake calmness. It had been ten days since he submitted his designs, and each day since then he'd hourly expected a call. In truth he'd expected a polite rejection; ten minutes after the designs were out of his hands he wanted them back, he wanted to make changes, lots of them. Why had he let them go without waiting a few days to let his objectivity develop? No man of mature judgement would have done that. But he had, and he'd waited and waited and hated himself for his haste.

'All of the design submissions for the Brauhaus project are with us, now.' Lamont pointed to a stack of mount boards and portfolios leaning on the wall by the window. 'They've been considered carefully. They've been argued over. I have to say that your designs had practically nothing in common with the others. And that's odd, considering the subject is one that's almost bound to bring out similarities of approach.'

Lamont went to the corner and picked up the folder

Colin had submitted. He brought it to the desk and opened it. Of the four designs Colin had done, the one he liked least was the one Lamont propped up beside him. Colin looked at it, feeling he was being accused of something.

'I'm intrigued,' Lamont said. 'I simply had to ask you, for my own satisfaction and that of our other directors – why did you settle on the folding money motif?'

'Is it that obvious?'

'Yes, it is. It shouts at you. It's so close to currency it looks like some kind of clever forgery.'

'Money seemed like a good analogy for the card, for what it does – what it means to the holder, I mean.'

'And you believe that would make men and women of substance want to possess such a card?'

'Yes,' Colin said, beginning to feel defensive. 'I do believe that.'

Lamont stared at the drawings for a moment. 'Didn't it occur to you that it's a rather, uh, *vulgar* motif? Brash, even? Un-subtle? Imagine what happens. Bright, sharp executives are shown a replica of money and they see the heavy-handed trick right away. "I'm really something special," the card yells. "I must be. I look like money, for Christ's sake." Did you really think the target group for the Brauhaus card would go for that kind of approach?'

So he'd been brought here for a drubbing, Colin thought. Not only a rejection, but a telling-off for his misguided approach. He wasn't sure the Milestone Agency was entitled to do that.

'I believe I was on the right lines, Mr Lamont. That's why the banknote style is the keynote of all four designs. I had faith in it.'

'I see.' Lamont put the drawing back in the folder. 'The other designers' submissions have one thing in common. All of them. They have opulence, *quiet* opulence, Mr

Russell. Taste. Some of them look almost too precious to touch. Our Managing Director was moved to say of one design that it's the most lusciously desirable card layout he's ever laid eyes on.'

Colin sighed. It was enough to be put down, without having his nose rubbed in other people's work.

'The consensus, briefly, is this.' Lamont leaned on the desk again, spreading his fingers on the lethal-looking edge. 'Your designs hammered the fact that this card is money, big money, not at all the kind of money that just any old wage-earner would have in his savings account. These designs . . .' He turned and tapped the folder. 'They support the philosophy that if you've got it, you should flaunt it.'

'Well, as I told you – '

'That philosophy, for better or worse,' Lamont interrupted, 'happens to be one of the mainstays of this organization. And of Brauhaus AG. We weren't asked to design for a firm of Bond Furriers, after all. This prestige card is going to be issued by a car parts organization. An awful lot of cars are blatant status symbols. There's a huge flaunt market out there, and in our collective view, your designs could help to make substantial inroads on that market.'

Colin blinked, trying to unravel what Lamont had just said.

'I'm telling you the job's yours, Mr Russell.'

It soaked through a word at a time. Colin straightened in his chair.

'I've got it?'

Lamont nodded. 'The way you've grasped the specification and pinpointed the character of the product is highly impressive. You caught the point the others missed, and you grasped it with flair. That's why we're happy to award you the commission.' Lamont tapped the folder again. 'There's work to be done, mind you. We've a whole list of suggestions – well, they're directions, actually. How you interpret them is up to you, of course.' Lamont looked at his watch. 'How are you fixed for time?'

'I'm at your disposal,' Colin said.

'Good. I think if I can get one or two of my colleagues in here we could thrash out some of the groundwork on the revisions. Then, perhaps, you'll go away and think about them for a while, then bring us some tentatively updated layouts as soon as you can. Does that suit you?'

'Just fine,' Colin said, almost tempted to confess that he'd crawl across broken glass in the process, if they found that necessary.

'Splendid.' Lamont sat down behind the desk and picked up the telephone. 'How does it feel, landing the commission against some of the best competition there is?'

'I'm – I'm . . .' Colin cast about in his head, trying to find words to express what he truly felt. 'Shattered,' he finally said. 'Marvellously shattered.'

The sensation lasted all day. He suspected it might last the rest of the week. Even his mother's tepid response to his news did nothing to scrape off the bloom. Colin felt good.

'I'm going out for an hour or so,' he told Ena when she'd finished watching her favourite TV soap. 'There's a man I want to see about something. Are you going to be all right on your own?'

'I don't see why not.'

Since spending two days in hospital, Ena now affected an invalid's air, even though they had done so much to balance her condition that she was now much better than she'd been for months.

'You've got the phone, remember,' Colin said, pointing

to the brand new extension that sat on the table beside her chair. 'The Paxton's number's on the pad. If you need to at all, for any reason, just give them a ring and they'll send me running. Aunt Joan's number's there too, if you feel like having a natter. There's your hot pad for your ankles and a spare cushion if you want it, down there on the bottom shelf of the table.'

He went to the hall and came back with his windcheater. 'You've no need to get out of your chair, remember.'

'Unless I want the loo,' Ena said grumpily.

'You went hardly more than half an hour ago,' Colin said. 'You'll not need to go before bedtime. I know you by now, Mum.' He kissed her cheek. 'Shan't be too long.'

'Enjoy yourself,' Ena grunted, hitting a button on the television remote control. 'It must be nice to go out when you feel like it.'

When Colin got there the Paxton was crowded. Friday, by recent tradition, was the pub's busiest night of the week. Saturdays were busy too, but nowadays the young contingent tended to wander out of the district and find places where they could drink and be entertained right through until Sunday morning; of the older men, perhaps half the number who used to have a Saturday night in the pub now spent it at home with an off-licence take-away and the TV set.

Gavin, the landlord, stood shaking his head as Colin squeezed in at the bar and paid for his pint.

'The telly's ruined everything, Col,' he said. 'Just look at this place.'

'Seems busy enough to me,' Colin said. 'It's taken me five minutes to get close enough to order a drink.'

'That's the whole point. It's too bloody busy. An' tomorrow it'll not be busy enough. We used to have a *balance*, mate. Folk had set ways and we had some kind of regularity in our trade. But now the telly drives stacks of them out on a Friday and keeps stacks of them in on Saturday. Tuesdays an' Thursdays have gone a bit odd, an' all. Television's the biggest blight to human behaviour since the invention of the motor car.'

The mention of cars put a little spur behind Colin's buoyancy. Cars equalled status, status equalled fancy credit cards, fancy credit cards equalled a nice windfall for Colin Russell, esquire. His self-confidence, which had been dragging badly just lately, had gone on the climb. He took a good swallow of beer and jerked his thumb at the crowd behind him.

'Is Andy Riordan anywhere among that lot?' he asked Gavin.

'Yeah, somewhere.' Andy pointed to the far end of the bar. 'He was up there with his missus about ten minutes ago.'

'Cheers.'

Colin pushed his way along the bar, nodding to people he knew, holding his glass close to his chest as collective exuberance and merriment created tidal waves among the clientele. When he got to the far corner he saw Andy at once, leaning on the wall by the cigarette machine. He was being talked at by his diminutive wife.

'Colin! Nice to see you, mate!' Relief swept Andy's face. He had clearly been having a hard time, with nobody to turn to for rescue. 'Bunty, you remember Colin Russell, don't you?'

Bunty turned and looked at Colin. She had naturally clenched features that clenched a little tighter as she tried to place the face.

'Oh, yeah. We were at school at the same time. Your dad was a builder with the council, like mine was, right?'

'That's it,' Colin said. 'But you weren't called Bunty at school, were you?'

'Beryl,' she said, making a mouth. 'My real name.'

'So tell us how things are goin', Colin,' Andy said, anxious to hang on to his company. 'Have you done anythin' about that credit card job?'

'I'll say I have.' Colin reached in his pocket and took out an envelope. 'What do you think of those?'

Andy opened the envelope. It contained four card-size colour reproductions of the designs Colin had done for Milestone. Andy spread them between his hands, shaking his head.

'Je-sus. These are somethin' else, Col . . .'

'They're just what you suggested,' Colin said. 'I took your specificaton to heart.'

'Are you serious?' Andy looked at Bunty, who was frowning at the cards. He looked at Colin again. 'You're telling me I put ideas like this into your head?'

'Yes, you did.'

'Is that what you do, then?' Bunty asked. 'Draw credit cards an' money an' stuff like that?'

'Sometimes. I met Andy in here one night about a couple of weeks ago. I wasn't sure how I'd go about this particular project, but he put me right.'

'He never put anybody right about anythin' in his entire flamin' life,' Bunty said flatly. She glared at Andy. 'What had you been drinkin' that night, then? Must've been somethin' good.'

Andy was about to launch into a defence and explanation of himself when a woman called Bunty from along the bar. Bunty waved and after an exchange of lip-readable messages with her friend she told Andy she was going across to have a word.

'I haven't seen her in ages. I won't be long.'

Andy watched Bunty go. 'Thank God for a bit of distraction,' he said. 'She was really givin' my earhole a bashin'. Money again, of course. That woman worships money. I mean they all like the stuff, but Bunty's made a religion out of it.'

'It's money I want to talk to you about,' Colin said, seeing Andy's face immediately go cagey. 'Mind if we go over and lean on the bar? I need a lean when I'm drinking, if I can't get a seat.'

They crossed to the corner of the bar and set down their glasses. Colin propped an elbow on the mahogany and put his foot on the brass rail.

'That's better.'

'Money, you said,' Andy murmured. 'In what way, like?'

'Those designs – I sent them in to the agency. Then I waited and waited. Today I got the word. The commission's mine.'

'Oh, great,' Andy said, still not understanding.

'There's a decent bit of cash in it for me. I want to cut you in. It's only fair, I reckon. You really did put the spark in me.'

'Oh, I don't know, mate,' Andy gestured like a man passing off an accomplishment lightly. 'All I did was tell you what I thought. I thought a card should look like gelt. The work, well that was down to you, wasn't it? The really hard bit, I mean. All I did was shoot the breeze, like I'm always doin' anyway.'

'There's people make a good living out of what you did for me,' Colin pointed out. 'I'm not offering you a huge share, mind you. I'm not daft. But I want to show my appreciation.'

Andy still looked reluctant. Colin could put himself in the other man's place; to men like Andy, it must seem very dodgy to be offered hard cash for a casually uttered opinion.

'What kind of money are you talkin' about, Colin?'

'Two hundred quid. Call it a consultancy fee.'

'Aw, Colin, you're jokin!'

'You *deserve* it, Andy.'

Andy was shaking his head. 'I'm not sayin' I couldn't use the money. With a wife an' a business like mine, I'm always on the lookout for extra bunce. But this . . .' He snatched up his glass suddenly and emptied it into his throat. 'Let's have another drink an' talk it over. I need to get used to the idea.' He shook his head again. 'No. I need to get to like the idea.'

'I'll get the drinks,' Colin said, grinning.

It was at that point, or a few seconds later as Colin was setting a fresh pint in front of Andy, that Bunty came back, bringing her friend and her friend's husband. Introductions were made. The friend was Irma, a square little woman in her late thirties with so much frizzy hair it made her face look unnaturally tiny. Dan, her husband, was tall and balding, with a hooded expression that suggested he wasn't too happy about being there.

'Dan's a policeman,' Bunty said. 'Hope you've both been behavin' yourselves.'

Andy immediately looked wary, even though his mouth was curled in a smile. Colin shook hands with the couple and offered to buy them a drink. Irma said she'd love a half of lager and blackcurrent. Dan fancied a pint of lager, if Colin didn't mind.

'We've been havin' an argument,' Irma explained as the drinks were being ordered. 'Me an' Dan, that is.' She threw her husband an old-fashioned look. 'He's got some funny notions.'

'You're the one with the funny notions,' Dan said, making it sound like a caution. 'Live and let live. We'd all be in a fine mess if we thought that way. Where do you draw the line, for God's sake?'

'He wanted to move as soon as *they* came in,' Irma said.

She pointed with a chubby finger. Two men with thick, carefully-clipped moustaches and short haircuts were standing halfway along the bar. They wore almost identical checked lumberjack shirts, jeans and trainers.

'What's wrong with them?' Bunty asked. 'I mean apart from lookin' like twins.'

'They're vermin,' Dan snapped. He took the pint Colin had bought him. 'Cheers.'

'How come?' Bunty insisted. 'Crooks, are they?'

'Worse than that.'

Colin was sipping his drink, doing his best to become a passive presence. Andy was looking at the two men, who seemed to be enjoying an ordinary conversation.

'They're known as Castro clones,' Dan said darkly. 'Named after a district in San Francisco. A *gay* district. Gay, indeed.' He tutted. 'Most miserable-looking shower of degenerates you ever saw. They wouldn't be called Castro clones if I'd my way. Castrated clones, more like.'

'Oh.' It had dawned on Andy. 'Poofs.' He sniffed. 'I don't mind them, meself, as long as they don't bother me.'

'They can be hilarious company,' Bunty said. 'There used to be two of them came in the Baker's Arms. They were a real hoot.'

'They're no laughing matter,' Dan snapped. 'They're the scum of the earth. They put up this harmless, sweetie-sweetie front, or you get the other kind, *that* kind, all manly and civilized, when all the time they're giving in to weaknesses and perversions that'd get any other person ten-to-fifteen. But we're an enlightened country, aren't we? We went and legalized them.'

'Well,' Andy said, 'when you think about it, there has to be a lot of exaggeration about what they get up to, hasn't there? It's human nature for folk to invent what they don't know about.'

'I'm a police officer,' Dan reminded him, 'and I don't have to invent anything. There's things I know about that kind I couldn't bring myself to repeat, whatever the company.'

'Men an' women get up to some pretty hairy antics,' Bunty said, 'if the hints in some of the court cases you read are anythin' to go by. It'd fair turn your stomach, some of it.'

'Not the same thing at all,' Dan said, gulping more lager.

Conversation was shut off for a moment as they all looked at the two men again. Colin felt that if Dan had known anything about him, he would have regarded him as a spy in the enemy camp. Except these people weren't the enemy. He could never feel they were, not even big Dan with his cemented prejudices. What Colin really felt like, underneath his chameleon skin, was a man isolated by other people's unwillingness to accept. He meant no one harm and he bore no hatred towards any living soul. Yet people could easily hate him, given the unremarkable facts.

'Old Colin here,' Andy said, as they tore their attention away from the two men along the bar, 'he's a – what is it, Col? An art designer – '

'Graphic designer.'

'Yeah, that's it, graphic designer. Well, you'll get a few of them kind in your line, won't you? Art, dancin', the theatre, they all seem to get more'n' their share, don't they?'

Colin found himself the unwilling focal point. He shrugged slowly, as if he hadn't given the matter much thought. Then he thought to hell with it – why should he duck and weave all the time? That could draw as much suspicion as anything.

'You don't know what people are really like, do you?'

he said. 'I mean certain characteristics are brought out by certain jobs. Art and dance and acting, they're outgoing activities. They attract scrutiny. But it's just as likely, I think, that there are gays in every walk of life. Plenty of them.' He offered Dan a chummy, jokey smile. 'Gay bobbies, even.'

Dan grunted. 'That'll be the day.'

'Dennis Nilsen was a constable.'

Dan frowned at his glass, then at Colin. 'Not for long,' he said, issuing the caution again.

'But I think there's a reason why so many people who aren't like the majority go into the theatre and the arts.' Colin had started on his thread of exposition and thought he might as well finish it. 'Acting and dancing and drawing pictures – writing books, for that matter – they all offer an escape from reality. If the world imposes a kind of reality on you that doesn't suit, or that actually causes you pain, you're apt to want an alternative, aren't you?'

'Christ Colin,' Andy said, 'that was a bit steep for a Friday night in the Paxton.'

'You can see what he means, though,' Irma said. 'It makes sense, doesn't it?'

'It doesn't change the facts.' Dan gave Colin a very hard look before he ran his gaze round the others. 'Homosexuals are an abomination. Nothing less. We've made light of them for years, made a joke of them, let them carry on with their corruption and filth, and see where it's landed us.'

'AIDS, you mean?' Andy said.

'Precisely. AIDS. The foulest, most deadly disease there's been in the whole history of mankind. And *they* presented us with it. They cooked it up with their corruption. It's the human equivalent of Dutch Elm disease. You'll see.'

'I reckon the boffins'll get a cure,' Andy said.

'Maybe,' Dan said, making it clear he believed nothing of the sort. 'But prevention's far, far better than cure. We should have taken the preventive measures long ago. But we're too enlightened for that. Enlightenment will be the death of us.'

Irma jiggled her drink. 'I wish we could talk about something less serious. I came out to enjoy myself.'

To Colin's relief, Andy launched into a description of his new batch of market lines. Pretending to listen as avidly as the two women, Colin let his eyes flick occasionally in Dan's direction. The big copper had clocked him, he believed. The closet door wasn't very far open, but some people were trained to peer through chinks.

'Personal planners,' Andy was saying, 'beautiful jobs, they are. One of them'd be just up your street, Colin. Black lockable PVC wallet, with a pen, ruler an' calculator inside, an' a diary, notebook – the lot. Then there's these survival tools. Never know when you'll need one of them. One day you find yourself in the wrong place when Milwall's playin' at home. The tool's got a knife, scissors, things for gettin' you out of police horses' hoofs . . .'

Andy droned on. Colin could feel big Dan's suspicion taking a lock on him. He should have kept quiet, stayed passive. *INVITE NO ATTENTION!* That was a rule and he should have stuck to it.

'Andy . . .' Colin interrupted apologetically, making a show of looking at his watch. 'I've got to be going. Mum's on her own and she's not been too well.'

'Oh, that's tough, Colin.'

'Yeah, well . . .'

Colin moved away from the bar, imagining the questions coming from Dan as soon as he had gone. 'Is your mate a bachelor, Andy? Lives with his mum, just the two of them at home, is that the picture?'

'Give your mother my best wishes,' Andy said. 'I'm sure she remembers me.'

'I'll do that.' Colin took a sealed envelope from his pocket. 'Here's that bit of business we were talking about. I hope a cheque's all right.'

Andy hesitated, his hand halfway to the envelope.

'Take it,' Colin said. 'I'll feel a lot better if you do.'

Andy took the envelope, mumbling something. Colin said goodnight to the women and to Dan. Dan nodded stiffly.

Outside, Colin paused, gathering his sense of himself about him again. He'd had a good day, he reminded himself. He had made headway, so there was cause to feel good. Sod what had happened in there – it was nothing anyway. So maybe one more bloke had weighed him up. So what? He'd had enough years to know how a black man feels in Alabama.

Walking home, keeping his stride brisk, he began to feel the glow come back. He'd made it, against some big competition. He'd proved himself. That was something to print across his mind and stare at every so often. His work, God bless it, had seen him through again. Work and work alone sustained him and gave his existence meaning and fulfilment.

The good glow carried him round the corner. It warmed him across the road. Then it left him, abruptly, as he spotted cousin Elaine's car parked at the gate.

7

If Auntie Joan could be compared to Alfie Bass – and she could, by even a charitable observer – then her daughter was a dead ringer for Elton John. It was an observation Colin could never escape. He saw the pair rarely, so the resemblances came as a fresh little shock each time. There must have been a glut of male genes or hormones in Joan's family chemistry; nothing else could have explained it. Elaine, with her short nose set at its stubborn angle, her broad forehead and firm mouth, could be expected at any minute, Colin swore, to break into a soulful rendering of *Candle in the Wind*. Except she only looked like the singer. Behind all that there was a woman with more than male hormones pounding in her blood; it was Colin's belief, he'd once told Bill, that a lot of vinegar circulated in Elaine's angular body.

They were in the living room when Colin came in. Joan sat opposite Ena at the fireside and Elaine was perched on the edge of the couch. Colin caught reproach in Joan's expression and the usual disapproval in Elaine's.

'Hello,' Colin said, taking off his windcheater. 'This is a surprise.'

'We dropped over to see your mother,' Joan said. She looked at Ena with wide, anxious eyes. 'I had this feeling I had to come, somehow. Right in the middle of Friday Night is Music Night – we always listen to that, Elaine and me – I had this, I don't know, it was kind of a premonition.'

Colin smiled. 'Your premonition equipment must be on

the blink, then. Mum's fine, as you can see. Aren't you, Mum?'

After a moment's hesitation Ena nodded. She wasn't keen to acknowledge she was a lot better these days.

'She doesn't look particularly fine to me,' Elaine said.

Her voice had the schoolroom ring, Colin thought. People who lorded it over children all day tended to believe they had natural authority in the real world.

'How do you mean?' Colin put his jacket on a chair and pushed back his sweater sleeves. 'The doctor's very pleased with her.'

'She doesn't look well enough to be left sitting in here all on her own.'

'I was only out for a little while.'

'He likes his nights in the pub,' Ena said, getting the mixture of charity and rebuke just right. 'I don't know where you'd be without that pub, eh, Colin?' The smile was thin and pained.

'Well . . .' Colin shrugged at Elaine and spread his hands. 'What can you do, when you've got a habit like mine to feed? I suppose I could get drunk at home, but it's not the same, somehow.' He turned and made for the kitchen. 'Tea, anybody? Coffee?'

Apart from himself nobody wanted anything. At the sink Colin filled the kettle and wished he'd stayed in the Paxton a while longer. Big Dan's glowering suspicion was nothing beside the synchronized censure of the Hags of Chiswick. He knew why they were here, and it had nothing to do with premonitions or even genuine concern for Ena.

They were bored. These occasional night-time visits occurred always at the tail-end of the winter, when Joan and Elaine were still months away from their Eastbourne holiday. They had few relatives, fewer friends, and nobody ever called on them. Friday night came, it got dark early and they felt shut in. So they piled into Elaine's car and inflicted themselves on somebody. Because of recent events, who better to land on tonight than Ena? There was the bonus of having a moan at Colin. They couldn't weigh him up, so he was an irritant – and they had to let him know he was.

As he stirred his tea Colin decided he wasn't going to take any flack off the girls this evening. Life leaned only on the people who didn't shove back. Over the years he'd put up with enough of his aunt's guidelines on living and his cousin's pathetic attempts at intellectual supremacy. And apart from all that, he just felt like annoying those two cows for putting a rancid end on what had been a particularly good day.

'So how's tricks, Elaine?' he asked brightly as he went back to the living room. 'Spreading enlightenment with as much vigour as ever?'

'I'm still trying,' Elaine said, not meeting his eyes. She rarely met his eyes. 'The atmosphere in public-sector education's a bit turbulent, at present.'

'So I've been reading.'

Colin decided against sitting down. Instead, he leaned on the wall by the sideboard, where he could see and address all three women easily.

'And what have you been doing, Colin?' Joan asked, perhaps sensing she should divert his attention from Elaine. 'Still trying to struggle along on your own?'

'Oh, I stopped struggling. It happened round about the time I went out on my own, as a matter of fact. I have to work hard, but I'm doing rather well.'

'I suppose you will be, come to think of it. I mean you see so many showcards all over the place these days. I suppose you're kept busy painting them all the time.'

Her ignorance of what he did was a sham, of course. Colin had known that for years. His aunt belittled people's occupations and professions automatically, just as she constantly elevated her daughter's calling to the level of an art at which only a few – Elaine supreme among them – could hope to succeed.

'I don't paint signs or showcards, Auntie.'

'Oh, I thought that was your job.' The level of surprise in her voice suggested shock. 'You used to do that though, surely? I've seen your little drawings and other bibs and bobs, advertising things . . .'

'Colin's a designer,' Ena said.

'Oh, well . . .' Joan shrugged. 'You can give jobs special names, of course, just to lend them a bit of dignity – and I don't see why people shouldn't do that, mind you. Don't misunderstand me.'

'It's all right,' Colin said. 'I don't misunderstand you. That window over there's not as transparent as you are.'

He saw Elaine stiffen. Her mother's head did a little waggle. Ena stared at him.

'As it happens,' Colin continued smoothly, 'designer is the basic name for my occupation. Fancier names are applied to it – Creative Stylist is one, Graphic Parameter Originator is a really far-out one. But I don't go in for fancy labels.' He smiled at Elaine. 'They do it in your profession, don't they? All it does is cause confusion. I don't like labels at all, actually. People are too keen to label other people. I don't think of myself so much as a graphic designer, as a person who makes graphic designs.'

'But, um,' Joan said, her voice choked, 'that's still about making little drawings, isn't it? I mean I wasn't getting it wrong, what you do, was I?'

She was stinging from the remark about her transparency, Colin noticed. She had gone purplish pink. He had been deliberately blunt, because that was one thing she could never be. Joan dropped hints, snide remarks, innuendos. Bluntness had to be avoided at all costs, because her kind weren't equipped for battle in the open.

'I suppose you could say that,' Colin said, 'as long as you can also say that being a doctor is about giving people prescriptions, or teaching children is about reading to them from books.'

'There's more to it than that!' Joan snapped huffily.

Colin nodded. 'I know. And there's more to my job than drawing pictures – big or little.'

'I've never understood much about it,' said Ena, trying to bring down the tension and simultaneously warning Colin with her eyes. 'I'd have said you were an artist, and that's that.'

'Oh no, I wouldn't call myself an artist.'

Colin began to wonder about himself. He had come in from the kitchen intending to be needly, but he hadn't expected to get so much of a buzz from it. He was *dying* to wade into Joan and Elaine.

'An artist, in the strict sense, creates freely and doesn't have to obey too many rules. And he creates his own guidelines. Artists are superior to designers in lots of ways.'

Joan bit the bait. 'The ones I've seen on television look inferior to most people, never mind to designers. Scruffy hairies.'

'Decadent, the half of them,' Elaine said, nodding.

'I'm not acquainted with a millionth of them, let alone half,' Colin said, 'so I wouldn't know about that. As for a bit of decadence – well, I'm not against that. I quite enjoy it, occasionally.'

'Maybe you're more of an artist than you think,' Elaine said sharply.

'I'm just human, Elaine. Real human beings are decadent a lot of the time. Ask one.'

Colin sipped from his mug, getting the glimmer of a suspicion that he was attacking two aggravations – the domestic intrusion of his relations, and the near-certainty – from his brief meeting with Dan the copper – that yet one more pair of bigoted eyes was fixed on him. The explanation didn't excuse his urge, though. It was aggressive, and aggression was the slipway to violence. Colin hated violence. Yet here he was, spoiling for a fight he knew he could win – which put him in the bewildering position of being a bully.

'I think I'll have a cup of tea after all,' Ena said. 'I've got the tingles again. A hot drink helps them. How about you, Joan? Elaine?'

Joan shook her head.

'I don't want to impose,' Elaine said.

'A bit late for that, I'd have thought,' Colin said, heading for the kitchen again.

The telephone by his mother's chair rang. Colin paused and waited while she answered it.

'Mrs Russell here.' A pause, nodding. 'Yes, he's here. Hang on, he's coming.' Ena put her hand over the mouthpiece. 'It's for you, Colin. Some girl called Mandy.'

Colin came and took the receiver. Joan stared at him stonily. Elaine glared.

'Hello? Mandy?'

Her voice was muted. 'I'm sorry to bother you, Colin.'

'Don't be sorry. It's no bother. Is something wrong? You sound kind of subdued.'

'I've had a bit of a – oh, an upset.' She paused and Colin could hear her shaky breathing. 'Colin, I know it's a cheek, but could I talk to you? Tonight? I wouldn't ask if it wasn't so important . . .'

Colin thought for a moment. 'Yeah,' he said. 'Why not. It's the same address as before?'

'Yes.'

'It'll take me about ten minutes.'

'Bless you, Colin.'

'See you in a bit.'

He put down the receiver and turned to his mother. 'Are you going to be all right on your own for a while? Say an hour or so?'

Ena made her hurt face. 'I suppose so. Joan and Elaine are here. Maybe they'll stop a bit longer.'

'Of course we will,' Joan said. 'Can't have you being here all on your own again.'

Colin took his jacket from the chair and put it on, his head loaded with retorts. But the impulse to wound had gone. The witches were serving a purpose now. He crossed and kissed his mother's cheek.

'Is there something up?' she asked.

'I'm not sure. I'll find out when I get there.'

Colin waved a light goodbye to his aunt and cousin and headed off into the hall. The front door opened and banged shut. Ena looked at the other two. Elaine was showing stiff affront; Joan was wreathed in disapproval again.

'So there *is* a woman in the picture,' she said thinly.

'It seems so,' Ena murmured, looking thoughtful. And uneasy.

The flat was small, cosy and simple. In the white-walled sitting room a pair of low-backed grey armchairs faced a matching two-seater couch near the fireplace. There was a long blue-grey sideboard with books and a drinks tray on top. Ten steel-framed pieces of original artwork – three of them Colin's – were arranged in two even rows along one wall. A narrow bookcase housed a collection of big, expensive books: three volumes on Japanese packaging, the album of the Creative Club of Belgium, the French *Le Livres des Illustrateurs* for 1985, plus an exotic collection of American, Swiss and Scandinavian art directories. Above the fireplace, in a slim-edged gilt frame, was a pencil sketch of a man. It was obviously a picture that was important to Mandy.

She was in a long blue dressing-gown and slippers. Her hair was tied up higher than usual and there was no trace of make-up on her face. As she brought Colin into the sitting room he noticed the set of her shoulders was different; she walked like someone defeated.

'Thank you for coming.'

'It's all right,' Colin said. 'You did me a favour. There's a couple of people at home who were bringing out the worst in me.' He watched Mandy sit on one of the armchairs. He sat on the couch opposite and leaned his elbows on his knees. 'Tell me, then. What is it?'

'Oh . . .' Mandy put a hand to her eyes, as if she was shielding them from a strong light. Her mouth opened and closed a couple of times, then she said, 'I'm almost sorry I asked you to come, now. Laid out plain it must sound so sordid . . .'

'If it does, I'll stop you,' Colin said softly.

'It's man trouble . . .'

'I've had some of that, in my time.'

Mandy clasped her hands around her knees. 'It's gone on for a year. Thirteen months, actually. It didn't start easily, I put up a lot of resistance. But he was persuasive. And patient – I wish to God he hadn't been so patient with me. If he'd given up . . .'

'Take it from the start, Mandy. Easy stages, if you like.'

'We met at one of those product launches you always avoided,' she said. 'He's the financial director of an up-market leisure-wear company. A gifted man, very cultured, terribly good looking.'

'Sounds like the perfect bloke,' Colin said. He pointed to the picture above the fireplace. 'Is that him?'

Mandy nodded. Colin studied the picture. The man had open, confident features. In the picture he was smiling; it looked as if he could do that with great charm and ease.

'The perfect bloke,' Mandy said, echoing Colin. 'Forty years old this year, just ten years older than me. Even the age gap is perfect. What isn't perfect, though, is that he's married. Has been since he was twenty-five. That's what made my resistance set in – if he'd been single it'd have been a whirlwind job. Anyway, he persisted. He made no bones about the marriage. He admitted it to me almost from the start and I believed him when he said it was far from ideal.'

'He wasn't happy?'

'The marriage wasn't enough. Sounds selfish, doesn't it? Wanting his cake and eating it. But it didn't sound selfish the way he put it to me. It sounded reasonable, I swear it did. What's more, as time passed the proposition began to look very reasonable and even desirable from my own point of view. You know me – I never saw myself as the marrying kind. An affair that wasn't in danger of deteriorating into marriage was the ideal. A nice, balanced, steady relationship that wouldn't infringe on my personal or professional freedom.'

'So you gave in.'

'Yes,' Mandy said. 'I gave in willingly. And for almost a year I was very happy. He was happy too, or I thought he was. He was a good husband – what his wife didn't know wouldn't hurt her, and he certainly gave her plenty of his time and affection. The children, too. He's got a boy and girl. Smashing kids.'

'You've seen them?'

'Once. In Regent's Park. I couldn't resist the opportunity of taking a look at his family. They were at an open-air concert. I knew they were going to be there, him too, so I got myself some big sunglasses and a floppy hat for a disguise, and I went to the park and took a good look. The children are the image of his wife. She's beautiful. A very serene girl. And devoted – that showed a mile off.'

Colin was staring at the carpet, his eyes distant as he pictured the arrangement.

'It does sound a bit sordid, doesn't it?' Mandy said. 'A married man, living comfortably down in Kent, with a family snug around him. A family that adores him. And all the time he's carrying on an affair with me. His up-front life's been a fake, and I've been a big part of the fake – his conspirator.'

'It doesn't sound sordid, particularly,' Colin said. He looked at Mandy. 'What I can't understand is how you could put up with it. Sharing him. Knowing you were sharing him with a woman who loved him.'

'I didn't see it as sharing, Colin. I had the separate part of his life. I had it exclusively. That was enough, you see. I didn't want all of his life. That kind of commitment is too much for me.'

Colin nodded slowly. 'So what's happened?'

'Just after Christmas, he hit me with a bombshell. He was going to leave his wife. He couldn't go on with the double life, he said. It was tearing him apart. I was shocked, of course. I asked him what he planned to do. He said he wanted to divorce her and marry me.'

'Hell's bells,' Colin sighed. 'I think I'm ahead of you.'

'I tried to explain,' Mandy said. 'I reminded him of what our arrangement was – he had his life, I had mine. There was a set area of common ground, a space we enjoyed. He said yes, he knew all that, but things had changed for him. He had fallen deeper and deeper in love with me. So much so he could hardly face his wife. I told him things hadn't changed for me. I still felt the same as before. I still cherished my freedom. I didn't want to marry him.'

'How did he take it?'

'Badly.'

'Did he get persuasive again?'

'Yes,' Mandy said. 'But this time I just got more stubborn. And I couldn't help thinking of his wife, going her sweet way through life, not knowing about the cliff edge up ahead. So finally, after a lot of arguing and tears, I finished with him.'

'When?'

'Today. This afternoon. I came back here tonight and soaked myself in the tub. I suppose I was symbolically washing him out of my life. Then I came in here, and I stood, and I felt this terrible, gnawing pain.' Mandy touched her heart. 'It was as real a pain as any. I realized what I'd lost.'

'And then you called me.'

'Yes. I had to talk to somebody. I had to communicate this terrible feeling I have. I could think of no one I could tell apart from you . . .'

'Because I'm bound to be objective?'

'Because I think I'd trust you more than anybody I know.'

Colin nodded. 'And you need me to talk you out of what you're tempted to do, because of this terrible feeling.'

Mandy sighed. 'You're a mindreader, too.'

'No, I'm just an expert.' Colin leaned back, smiling faintly. 'An expert's a person who's made all the mistakes. So I qualify.' He leaned forward again. 'You're tempted, against all the commonsense arguments, to make it up with the man, rather than suffer the terrible pain of loss. Right?'

'Three times I've nearly phoned him. I can be reasonably sane about the situation now, *right* now, because you're here. But when I'm alone . . .'

'I can only give you advice, Mandy. It's advice you've been trying to give yourself this evening – but maybe I can add something more convincing to it. Something to make you hang on.'

He stood up and walked a few paces across the room, then stopped and stared at the door, wondering how he could convey his own certainty. After a moment he came back and stood beside Mandy's chair.

'First, I'll say what's obvious. You'll ruin a woman's life if you do what you're tempted to do. You'll break her heart and hurt her children dreadfully. For what? Happiness? Not much chance of it, not with that kind of background. And not with the conditions your lover wants. The only reason for giving in to your impulse would be to get rid of the immediate pain, the tearing pain of loss.' Colin leaned close to Mandy. 'That pain will go by itself. So will the man's. And with any luck his marriage will be saved. His family will be rescued from an agony that would otherwise be certain. So the formula's simple. Do nothing. Wait. Just wait, and you'll heal.'

Mandy nodded. 'It makes sense.'

'Good sense is often hard to live by, mind you . . .'

Again Mandy nodded, her head drooping. 'I've got so used to him. To having him . . .'

'But what I say is right, isn't it? Tough or not, it's right.'

'Of course it is.' She said it wearily, as if acceptance was just one more pain and not an answer.

'Now I'll give you the extra bit of advice, the bit that might make things easier for you.'

Colin sat down opposite Mandy again. He reached forward and clasped her hands between his.

'Do you remember the way I used to go on about computer programs, how I was fascinated by the way they added to the machine's intelligence, giving it rules it would always obey, so long as they were stored in memory?'

'I remember,' Mandy said, smiling. 'You were obsessed with programs.'

'I think I still am, to some extent. They're soothing. I think that's because they're reliable. What I've tried to do, in the last couple of years or so, is program myself with reliable rules and make them such a fixed part of my intelligence and nature that I *have* to obey them. It doesn't always work, because I'm not as reliable or dispassionate as a computer. But most of the time, I manage to stick by the programs. There's one I'm very glad I took up. It's a two-word program. Hurt nobody.'

Mandy looked at him. 'That's a hard one,' she said.

'I'll say it is. And tonight I disobeyed it. I went out of my way to hurt two women, relatives of mine. Because, I suppose, in their way they're hurtful to me. But I shouldn't have tried to hurt back. I should have stayed well clear of any distress or annoyance they can cause me. That should have been the tactic of choice.'

'Do you find it pays, in general?' Mandy asked. 'Going out of your way to hurt nobody – it's not exactly sound business practice, is it?'

'It's great human practice, Mandy. I promise you, if you make a deliberate effort to avoid giving pain, of whatever kind, it makes changes in yourself you'd never believe. It's so good, in the long run, that it feels like selfishness.' He released her hands. 'Now's a good time for you to give it a whirl.'

Mandy stood, leaned forward and kissed Colin on the forehead. 'You're a good man. A good, good friend,' she said.

'I hope so. Promise me you'll take to heart what I've said. You'll hurt me, too, if you don't.'

Mandy's lips closed in a tight line for a moment, then she nodded firmly. 'I promise,' she said. 'I swear. Thanks, Colin. Thanks for coming, for listening, and for knocking a bit of sense into me. And I'm sorry for spoiling your evening with my troubles.'

'You've spoiled nothing,' Colin said. 'I've had a good day. Come to think of it, I've had one of my best days in ages.'

Mandy stepped back as he stood up. 'Tell me, Colin . . .'

'What?'

'Are you a happy man these days?'

'As happy as the likes of me can be, I suppose.' He stepped close, spreading his arms. 'Give us a cuddle before you kick me out, love,' he said. 'It'll make me that itsy bit happier still.'

8

At the beginning of March George Packer had an argument with one of the three directors associated with his touring theatre group. It was a serious argument, centring on George's continual upstaging of other actors and his refusal to take direction. The row began in a studio theatre in Hull at the end of a Tuesday-night performance. George stamped out while the director, Toby Markham, was still raging at him. The argument resumed when Toby tracked George to a Chinese restaurant in the centre of town.

'Walking out on me solves nothing,' Toby warned, slipping into the seat opposite George. 'This has got to get straightened out.'

George combed the fingers of one hand slowly through his hair, giving Toby his deeply-bored look.

'You have to get into line, George. You're upsetting the whole company and I'm not going to stand for that. You'll undermine this production just like you had a shot at cocking up our last two nights in Liverpool. Your fellow actors deserve better. It's no way to conduct yourself, as if you were in a one-man show.'

'Fellow actors,' George groaned. 'That bunch of low-talent, clodhopping dead-heads aren't actors. They're yobs and worn-out tarts playing at acting.'

Toby's red beard seemed to bristle as he leaned across the table. 'They're professionals, each and every one of them, with more pro discipline and pro know-how than you'll ever have.'

'Oh yes?' George tilted his head. 'And what West-End director is telling me this?'

'West-End directors reserve their opinions and judgements for West-End quality actors, George. I'm in provincial rep because it's where I belong and it's what I like.'

'Bully for you.'

'*And you're* with us because some misguided former committee member liked the length of your eyebrows, or something, and decided that made you an actor. You've got a contract which I can't really break, or I would. But I'll tell you this – your behaviour just lately leads me to believe it won't be long before you breach the contract yourself.'

A waiter came to the table. George ordered fillet beef cooked in ginger and a side order of fried rice. Toby asked for a plate of chow mein.

'Do join me, won't you,' George snapped. 'It's not enough I have to put up with you bleating at me in the theatre, I have to suffer it over dinner as well.'

'You'll suffer me until this is sorted out.' Toby unwrapped a Manikin and lit it. 'Now,' he said, blowing smoke towards George, 'I want a firm undertaking that you'll stop this posturing and larking about to distract the audience when other people are delivering their lines. And I want you to stick to the stage directions we agree at rehearsals.'

'I think I'm getting sick of this company,' George said.

'It's mutual. Now are you going to promise to come into line?'

George banged the side of his fist on the table, though not very hard. 'You're not talking to a bloody school kid!'

People at other tables were watching. George stared back haughtily until they had all looked away again.

'There's another thing, while I'm at it,' Toby said.

'And what would that be, dear heart?'

'Money.'

'Christ!' George slapped a hand to his heart. 'They're not putting our wages up, are they?'

'Don't play the fart, even if it is your best role,' Toby said. 'I'm talking about money you owe. Near enough seventy quid, to three separate members of the company.'

'That's none of your business.'

'They've made it my business. You've been pressed to return the cash, but you haven't been forthcoming. And there's the matter of borrowed clothes, too. A jacket here, a shirt there, a pair of boots – none of it given back.' Toby put his hands on the ends of the table and levered himself as close to George as he could. 'You're more trouble than ten faggots in a company, pal. And don't give me that "who, *me?*" look. It's in my power to ground you for the rest of this tour. Replace you and keep you roasting in the wings. It's vindictive, George, I don't like it, but if I've got to do that to make you knuckle under and start doing the right things by other people, then I'll sodding well do it.'

Now it was George who leaned forward. 'Like I said, hairy man, I'm getting sick of the company. Sick of mixing with the dregs. Sick to my guts with performing for hicks and yokels. I think I'll just up and split.'

Toby shook his head and grinned. 'Split, eh? In a pig's arse you will. You're permanently skint. You've got no other source of income but the company. Where in hell are you going to split to, big noise? The Young Vic? The RSC?'

'There are places I can go,' George said, trying not to sound defensive. 'I've got friends.'

'Lepers have more friends.'

'You don't believe me, do you?'

Toby stretched. 'No, I don't believe you. Other members of the company have families, acquaintances, friends.

You seem to have nobody. The only acquaintance you appear to have is that landlord who was pressing you, then the company, for payment of back rent on some bedsit you had before you joined us. You're a lone figure, George. And it doesn't surprise me. Ten minutes after somebody gets pally with you, they regret it.'

'My friends are all in London, as if it was any of your business. I've got one who's a successful designer. He'd see I was all right.'

'George, you're going nowhere. Not until you square up your debts – and there's the matter of your contract. I'm sure nobody's going to try very strenuously to hang on to you, but things have to be done by the book – even though I know it's not your style.'

George stood up suddenly. 'Bugger you!' he yelped, shaking back his hair. 'Bugger the entire plebeian, moth-eaten company!'

'Now, George, don't do anything you'll be sorry for . . .'

'I'm sure you'll be able to see to the bill, big-timer.'

'George!'

With a swaggering stride he'd copied from Peter O'Toole in *The Night of the Generals*, George swept across the restaurant and out on to the street. Toby sat staring at the half-open door, wondering if he should go after him. He decided he wouldn't. This was just a tantrum. Georgie-boy would be at the theatre tomorrow as usual. Toby would give him another bollocking then, on the principle that enough concentrated aggro would shove the arrogant thespian back into line. Meanwhile Toby would eat the chow mein *and* the beef and rice. Arguments and slanging matches gave him an appetite.

By the time Toby was halfway through his meal, George was heading for the coach station with his bulging suitcase and shoulder bag. When he reached the station he bought a single ticket for London, then went to a phone booth and dialled Colin Russell's number.

'Oh, hello . . . Is that Mrs Russell? Ah, well, sorry to trouble you. I was wondering if I might speak to Colin.'

Ena told him Colin was out.

'Oh dear.'

She asked if she could take a message.

'Not really, no. It's kind of complicated. I'll get in touch with him later. Sorry to have troubled you. 'Bye.'

He came out of the booth and looked at his watch. The coach would be leaving in twenty minutes. There was time for tea and a sandwich. Instead of warning Colin he was on his way back, he would surprise him. Colin liked surprises.

'You can live in a place most of your life,' Ena said to Mrs Howell, 'and still not get used to it.'

They stood on the corner by Super Save and watched the traffic growling past. Ena had been to pick up a repeat prescription from her doctor and Mrs Howell, an older but sturdier woman, had popped out for her shopping. As occasionally happened they had met on the street and were conducting a habitual condemnation of the world around them.

'The reason we never get used to this place,' Mrs Howell said, 'is because it's always changing. There's no landmarks nowadays. One month there's a chemist's on that corner over there, then the next thing you know it's a Paki cut-price. And the traffic's got so bad, I'm scared half the time to cross the road.'

'And if it's not the traffic you've to mind out for, it's muggers.'

'What a world.' Mrs Howell shook her head at the human predicament. 'Muggers and drug pushers and kids sniffing lighter fuel. What's happened to everything, eh?

Where did morality and neighbourliness go?'

'Same place as good newspapers and a decent pork sausage,' Ena said. 'I told the doctor this morning, he'd be best employed sticking every woman on the pill, so there'd be no more kids being born into this mess.'

'Still seeing the doctor regularly then, are you?'

Ena nodded. 'Ever since that do, when I ended up in hospital. I've got to get myself checked every other week, and there's my pills and capsules and God knows what else to keep getting and taking.'

'How are you feeling, though? Is the medicine doing you any good?'

'It's hard to tell. There's times I think it is, but other times I feel terrible. I'm just up and down, love. That's the way it is when you're a diabetic. Up and down, up and down.'

A woman in a flowered headscarf waved from the doorway of a shop further along the street. Mrs Howell waved back.

'That's my daughter. I better go and have a word with her. With a bit of luck she might take me home with her and give me a cuppa.' She touched Ena's arm. 'It's been lovely seeing you again. Keep well now, won't you?'

'I'll do my best,' Ena said. 'Ta, ta, love.'

She turned in the direction of home and suddenly remembered she hadn't told Colin about the telephone call last night. That was another cross she bore – her memory. It got shorter by the day. This morning she had made a shopping list, only three or four items, but things that had to be written down or she would forget them when she was out. And, of course, she forgot to bring the list with her.

At the pelican crossing she pushed the button and waited. An old man at the kerb gave her a cross look. Ena realized he must have pressed the button already.

What difference did it make? Two pushes made sure. She often gave the button a couple of jabs, to be certain the signal connected. Silly old duffer, she thought, looking at the man. With a small shock she realized he used to live on her street. He was younger than Ena.

Old age, she thought, stepping into the road as the traffic stopped and the green man came on. Why did people have to get old? It was such a sad falling off. They should get firmer with age, slower and kind of stately. But not feeble, wrinkled, vacant-looking. Forgetful. A dignified, vigorous old age would be guaranteed in an ideal world. Which this wasn't.

When she got to the far side of the road she stopped, feeling the familiar ache in her ankles. Five minutes more and she would be home. Then she could have a nice hot cup of tea, sit down and read the local paper for an hour or so. The prospect brightened her. She took the turning that led to the end of her road, ignoring the pains in her feet and calves.

Then something happened. A sound like a fly buzzing too close came and went, then Ena's vision swam.

'Oh, Lord . . .'

It was like the time before, when she had passed out in the kitchen. Her head was getting light. It felt hollow. She knew she was still walking, but she had no idea how. She couldn't feel her feet. Her eyes cleared and she saw the barrier at the pavement's edge. It was coming straight for her. Ena put out her hands to stop it and heard her handbag hit the ground.

The barrier struck her knuckles and kept coming. She met it with her body and spun, facing the other way and falling sideways. There was no feeling, only the lightness and the sense of everything moving around her.

'Here, missus, hold on . . .'

A man and woman were coming towards her, hands

outstretched. Ena saw them only for a second as she pitched forward, feeling pain tear across her shoulder, then dull coldness as her face struck the pavement.

All diseases run into one – old age. Colin had read that somewhere long ago, but it had only come back to him now, standing in the ante-room of the women's medical ward.

It was her diabetes again, the doctor had told him. Colin had no doubt that was true. But would it have thrashed her the way it did if she'd been twenty or thirty years younger? He had seen her for only a minute and that had been as much as he could bear. His mother looked like a seriously damaged old rag doll, even when they had washed the blood from her face and put her in a tidy white bed.

The doctor came back into the room while Colin was staring at a badly-designed scenic calendar on the wall by the desk.

'Her collar bone's definitely broken, Mr Russell. But the head x-rays are clear.'

'Is she in any pain?'

'For the moment, no. But there'll be some discomfort for a few weeks as the collar bone heals. In a woman her age broken bones are always a problem. Then there's the complications, because of the diabetes.'

Colin looked at the man, finding him annoyingly smug in his cocoon of understanding.

'How serious are the complications, usually?'

'Well, healing could be delayed, for one thing.'

'What else?'

The doctor flapped his hands against his coat. 'A hundred and one vexations attend old folk when they're getting over illness or injury.'

Colourfully put, Colin thought. The plain black and

white of it, though, was that his mother was going to be a real invalid for a long time. She would have pain and misery. Her days would be full of everything Colin had prayed she would be spared.

'When can she come home?'

'I think we'll keep her here for a week or so. We can't tell the extent of the trauma, yet. We'll monitor her until her system stabilizes.'

The doctor pulled the door wide, indicating he had said as much as he intended. He was a busy man and he had a style that made it evident. Colin was suddenly aware he was in the way. He stepped into the corridor.

'I'll bring her things this evening,' he said.

'Fine.'

The doctor nodded – it was a sharp, single movement of his head, cutting off contact. Colin turned and walked towards the main door, feeling very bad about leaving his mother here.

There was mail on the hall carpet when he got home. A letter from Bill for Ena, an invitation for Colin to join an insurance scheme, and a cheque from the Milestone Agency. He stood in the kitchen, staring at the pink slip which could be converted to so much money. Who could he tell? Who would he show it to?

He realized he was feeling sorry for himself. Sorrow for his mother had overlapped his own grey emptiness. For weeks he had known his existence was becoming fearfully void; he had steeped himself in work, nothing but work. No social life at all and only his mother for company. Now he didn't even have her. It was easy to see himself as a single man with a vengeance, the ultimate outsider.

'Pack it in,' he told himself.

He had to remember that work was enough. Plenty of people in Britain, millions of them, were without it. Nowadays the man with a job was in a position of privilege

– far from feeling sorry for himself, he should feel lucky.

He took off his jacket and hung it in the hall. Back to work, that was the thing. Back to what mattered. On the stairs he thought of his mother lying in the hospital bed and had to shake aside a feeling of panic. *She's all right.*

But she wasn't all right. The poor old soul was in hospital again, and this time she had a broken bone. A fracture was always serious. In an old lady, one who was never in good health, a broken collar bone was a disaster. Colin could foresee complications. There was no point in deluding himself. He'd heard stories . . .

The doorbell rang, pulling him from the edge of a black mood. He went downstairs and opened the door. The sight of George made his heart lurch.

'Surprise, surprise,' George said.

'My God. What are you doing here?'

'I've left the company. For the sake of my sanity and self-respect. Can I come in?'

Colin stepped back. George came into the hall and dropped his bags. He put his hands on his hips and grinned.

'Come through to the kitchen,' Colin said. 'I'll make you a coffee.'

'Cheers.'

It was ten minutes before Colin got himself under control. He jangled through the preparation of coffee, nodding as George talked breathlessly about the awfulness of the past weeks, the sheer misery of working with inferior people in ghastly conditions, for the kind of money a street sweeper would scorn.

Toughest of all, for Colin, was sorting out how he felt about this. He had struggled to put George from his mind. Every sound argument had been marshalled and put to the purpose of writing this young man out of his life. He was something disturbing in the past, a person set aside.

Yet here he was. Big as life and actually *here*, standing in the kitchen. The reality cancelled all Colin's mental striving to remove George Packer from his heart and thoughts. But should Colin give in to that? Should he accept that George, up close, meant as much as he ever had?

'The awful thing is, of course, that I've nowhere to live.'

The words cut across Colin's uneasy decision to let things drift for now, without any action on his part.

'What – you've no digs at all?'

'Nowhere. I couldn't afford to keep the old place on. So the up and down of it is, I'm on the streets. Squalid, isn't it?'

There was a spare room, of course. Colin's head spun, wondering if he should offer it. Just to solve the immediate problem, of course. Only for a few days . . .

'I don't suppose you know of anywhere, do you? Anything'll do, until I'm properly on my feet again. Can't afford much in the way of rent of course, but – '

'There's a room here.'

Mistake! Colin's mind turned on him the instant the words were out. *Terrible mistake!* But to see the gratitude spread across George's face was such a pleasure . . .

'Really?' George was beaming. 'What about your mother? I mean will she mind, or anything?'

'Mum's in hospital. She'll be there for another week yet, so there's no problem, really . . .'

What use was caution? Colin stared at George, wondering if he could ever, at a showdown, deny him anything. There were a dozen reasons why he shouldn't get involved again. Serious reasons. He was issuing an open invitation to pain and every shred of his reason told him he was a mug. But what did reason have to do with it?

9

'How long have I been here now?' Ena asked. Her face was waxy yellow against the pillow. 'I feel like I've had this sling on for a month.'

'It's five days now,' Bill said. He put the new Victoria Holt novel he'd brought on the locker and sat down by the bed. 'The time'll pass a bit faster when you get home.'

'If I get home.'

'Well of course you will.'

It was Bill's third visit. He saw no improvement in his mother, and the doctor's estimation of her condition had been cautious. He buffered every hopeful sign with the reminder that Ena was not as young as she'd been, and her general health wasn't particularly good. She was still being monitored. Healing in the collar bone would be slow.

'Colin's not here yet. You'd think he could get here on time, wouldn't you? It's not much to ask.'

'He's a busy bloke, Mum. He has to do all his own running and fetching these days, remember. I'm sure he won't be long.'

Bill glanced round the ward. It was hard to let his eyes settle for long. So many women of all ages, looking so ill. They were harrowing places, these compounds beyond the edge of ordinary living. Illness frightened Bill.

'I'm not going to be able to come after tonight,' he said. 'I've hung close to London as long as I can. I have to be in Blackpool tomorrow morning, and I'll be locked in the north for another week or so.' He leaned forward and patted Ena's hand. 'You'll be out of here by then.'

'Maybe.'

'Who came to see you this afternoon, then?'

'Oh, Joan was here for a little while. Had to rush off, though. Something to do with her day club work. God knows why she's got herself mixed up in something like that . . .'

'Here's Colin,' Bill said. 'He looks like he's been running.'

Colin bustled up to the side of the bed and put down a lumpy paper bag. 'Sorry, sorry . . .' He pecked Ena's cheek and slapped Bill's shoulder. 'I had a late delivery to make and I got stuck in the traffic on the way back.' He stood panting gently, gauging his mother's appearance. 'Any better tonight?' he asked her.

'I feel worse, if anything.' Ena nodded at the bag on the locker. 'What have you brought?'

'Apples. You said you fancied some, and the doctor says it's all right for you to have them.'

'The notion's gone off,' Ena grunted.

Colin sat down on the opposite side of the bed to Bill. 'I've got a nice surprise for you back home,' he told Ena.

'What?'

'It won't be a surprise if I tell you.'

Ena sighed and shifted her trussed arm awkwardly. 'You shouldn't have said anything, then. Now I'll be fretting, wondering what it is.'

'Oh, well . . .' Colin shrugged. 'You might as well know. It'll be something to look forward to. It's a video recorder.'

'What do I want with one of them? I wouldn't know how to work it.'

'That's what you said about the remote control TV set. Now you know more about it than anybody.'

Ena was determined not to be pleased by Colin's news. 'I've no use for a gadget like a recorder. They're for folk that are out and want to catch a television programme later on. I'm never out. So what's the point?'

Colin swapped patient looks with his brother. 'You'll be able to record one channel while you're watching another. You can build up a collection of programmes you want to see again – and you can see films from the video library whenever you want. They've got South Pacific – you know how much you liked that one.'

'Wasting your money,' Ena said. 'That's all you're doing.' She sighed at the curtain rail over the bed.

Thirty-five minutes passed in difficult exchanges. Finally a handbell rattled to tell visitors it was time to leave. Bill kissed Ena goodbye and promised he would send her a postcard as soon as he got to Blackpool. Colin said he would look in the following afternoon.

On the steps outside Bill admitted he thought his mother looked terrible.

'Old age looks so – fixed on her, now. Like she'd always been that way.'

'She didn't need the broken bone, that's for sure. It's like something vital in her got snapped.' Colin dug his hands in his pockets. 'I'm going to have to face it – she'll need looking after, and not just the way I've been doing. She'll need a nurse.'

'You reckon it's that bad?'

'I can see it coming. She's getting feeble, Bill. Not in her mind but everywhere else. Another fall – well, I don't want to think what might happen.'

'Nursing will cost.'

'So it'll cost.'

Bill looked at his watch. 'Do you fancy a drink?'

Colin looked at his own watch. 'I don't really have the time . . .'

'Neither have I,' Bill said. 'I suggested it because there's something I wanted to talk over with you. But it can wait.'

'Are you sure?'

Bill nodded. 'It's serious, but it'll keep. I'll be back in London in a couple of weeks or so. We'll have a chat then.' He held out his hand. 'Take care of yourself. I'll ring nearer the weekend and you can fill me in on how Mum's doing.'

They shook hands. For one blessed instant Colin felt the old power, the blanketing protectiveness of his big brother.

'Safe journey, Bill.'

Later, driving towards a North London pub he didn't want to visit, Colin ran the same sad pictures of his mother he ran every night. It was an alternative to thinking too far ahead. The here-and-now was stable enough, if patched with sadness. He was in charge of things, he was successful enough to use money where talent fell short and he had no shortage of sympathy. The time when money and caring weren't enough was not to be contemplated, so he contented himself with reminders that things could be worse, but weren't *yet*.

Ena wasn't the only problem, the only sadness. George was becoming a problem. George had always been a problem. Anybody on the outside could see it and think themselves lucky not to be involved. But Colin was involved and he couldn't look at things as clearly as people on the outside.

From good-natured friendship and open, unselfish intimacy George had gone back, in the space of a few days, to his old mercurial, calculated style. Colin had no doubt he was being led by the nose again, but there was little he could do about that, except hope. The hope persisted and was nothing new – one day George would change. Colin believed it somewhere in his head, somewhere undefined, behind cold reason and all the evidence that men like George didn't change, except to get worse.

Colin pulled in at a parking space ten yards from the pub. He got out, locked the car and walked slowly to the amber-lit swing doors, instinctively pulling up his collar. He paused at the doors, hearing the music, the laughter. Squaring his shoulders, he elbowed his way in.

Heads turned and eyes calculated. The place was busy, as it usually was, its horseshoe bar aswarm with young business types, older business and Civil Service types, theatricals and an abundance of hustlers and hangers-on. Colin moved slowly to the bar, trying to spot George without letting his gaze linger on any face for too long. Some people read too much into a lingering look.

There was no sign of George. A man in the same kind of zippered, canvas-look jacket George had worn that afternoon swung round on a stool and caught Colin's half smile. It immediately became a non-smile when Colin realized his mistake, but by that time the man had smiled back, showing healthy teeth and consummate self-possession. Colin moved on, finding a space at the bar where he could stare at nothing but rows of bottles until someone took his order.

After a couple of minutes sipping his lager he turned and looked around again. He had been told how places like this had changed since the dark days of the fifties, when men sat huddled at corner tables, eyes darting like ballbearings, fearful of being tagged or picked-on. By comparison this was emancipation. Most of the younger men here had come yodelling out of the closet long ago, and the older ones were happy to let their façades drop in such safe surroundings. Colin hated the place, as much as he disliked all the other hangouts where gay men or women foregathered to celebrate a solidarity they didn't – and never would – possess. The idea of individuality was suspended in here. Everybody pretended to be the same, and united. Which was crazy and dishearteningly false. Islands, by definition, could never be united.

Here and there the truth could be seen erupting. A young man near Colin was driving a wedge of lies and eye-signals into a relationship that looked far from happy, anyway. Elsewhere a businessman with a permanently laughing mouth and anxious eyes was trying to use cash to detain a companion whose attention was obviously wandering. The air was thick with treachery. Men trying to keep tabs on their women didn't know the half of it.

'Hi, Col.' A hand landed on Colin's shoulder. He spun and saw George, weary-eyed as he always managed to look in these places, as if he knew something everybody else didn't. 'I got detained by an old buddy. Or we detained each other, to be accurate – kicking around old times, you know how it goes. Time flies and you don't realize . . .'

'I'll get you a drink.'

'Cheers.'

They found a table and sat down. George, as usual, arranged himself artistically, Mr Devastatingly-Cool, one leg bent with the foot hooked on the spar of his chair, the other leg extended, the whole arrangement seeming to be supported by his shoulder blades on the chairback.

'I'd have been happier to meet you in the Paxton,' Colin admitted. 'I hate hanging around here on my tod.'

'God, you're so hung up.'

'Maybe I am.'

'You should do something about it. Try to hang loose.' George let out a bark of laughter. 'I must say, it's hard to imagine. You loosening up.' He laughed again. 'What sort of day did you have?'

'Same as usual. I worked, then I visited Mum in

hospital. How about you? Any job leads? Word of any digs?'

'Just for once,' George drawled, 'I didn't spend the day grubbing for work or trying to scrounge the loan of a roof over my head. I did something to improve the quality of life.'

'I'd have thought,' Colin said, 'that a job and somewhere to live would do a lot towards improving the quality of your life.'

George groaned. 'You remind me of the way my father used to go on. Only you sound older.'

'Common sense tends to sound middle-aged,' Colin said. 'That doesn't make it any less relevant or important.'

'Tut, tut, dearie, you're going all testy on me . . .' George leaned sideways and chucked Colin under the chin. 'I hope we're not warming up for another lecture on the special relevance of an orderly lifestyle in the present general climate of crumbling morale.'

'Aw, George . . .' Colin ran a hand across his hair, trying to press back the exasperation. 'Don't start playing the clown. I'm only saying you should get yourself straightened out.'

'People keep telling me that. And usually they're people a lot more screwed-up than I am.'

'I'm not talking about being screwed up. I'm talking about getting your life in order, getting the basics sorted out.'

'I've been trying to do that. Today, as I said, I did something different. Just for a change.'

'What?'

'I retraced my steps. Tried to get back to the fork in the road, you know?' George lifted his glass, set it down again, lifted it, put it down again, making a pattern of wet circles on the table. 'I feel I took a wrong turning somewhere. I went back among some people I used to know. I tried to revive the flavour – the enthusiasms of earlier times.'

Colin looked at him. 'You're only twenty-eight now,' he said. 'It's hardly an age to start sifting the sands of time in your wake.'

'It's never too early for re-appraisal,' George said, folding his arms. He glanced sidelong at Colin, smiling. 'I quote, of course.'

'Who?'

'You. You said it once and I never forgot it. I won't tell you the circumstances or your reason for saying it at the time, it'd only make an old fogey like you blush. But you said it. And today I acted on it.'

'So what did you learn?'

'That I was happiest when I was at RADA, even though I could hardly wait to get out of the place. I also found out that other people foresaw great things for me. A number of them still do. All in all, it was a pretty moving sort of day.' George paused, then added, 'Expensive, too.'

'Don't tell me,' Colin said. 'You're skint again.'

'As good as. A few drinks, lunch, a taxi – it all adds up.' He sighed, gazing across the room, then sat forward suddenly. 'Shit!'

'What's up?'

George didn't reply. Colin tried to gauge his line of vision. There was a crowd of men over near the door. Beyond them, someone was trying to get through.

'Who is it, George?'

'Let's just piss off. I'll explain later.'

George got to his feet. Colin did the same. They were making for the side door when one voice rang out above the others.

'Hoi! Packer! Just freeze it there!'

Colin saw a big man now, fearfully big and determined.

He was striding towards them, his boot heels thudding on the carpet.

'Sit down,' he shouted, eight feet from them. 'You, Packer, I'm talking to *you*.'

'Stay, Colin,' George hissed. 'For God's sake don't run out on me.'

He returned to the table and dropped back into his chair. Colin went with him, but remained standing. As the big man came close the full surge of his menace could be felt as much as seen. He had wide dark eyes, a nose that flattened towards the bridge and a thick-lipped, muscular-looking mouth.

'I just missed you at the last place,' he said, ignoring the stares of people around him. 'But one of your little friends told me where you'd gone.' He sat down, spreading heavy hands on the arms of the chair. 'Did you think you could hide in London?'

'Who said anything about hiding?' George's fingers twitched a beer mat nervously. 'I came back, that's all.'

'Leaving unfinished business, not to mention a lot of chaos and inconvenience.'

George stared at the table.

'You're a right bastard, Packer.'

Colin picked up his glass, which was still half full. The man looked at him. Colin did his best to return the stare.

'Do you have business with this one?' the man demanded.

'He's a friend,' George snapped. 'Colin, this is Laurie Chilton. Stage manager and set designer for the company I was with up north.'

He was the least theatrical man Colin had ever seen. He looked more like a stevedore.

'I'll fill you in, shall I?' Chilton brought his hands forward and laid them on the table, ignoring Colin now.

'You walked out, or ran out, and it put us in a mess. We had to re-schedule, put in a deputy, screw around in eight directions before the curtain could go up. That was bad enough, but you went away with property belonging to other members of the company. You also owed money. After some discussion, we decided you wouldn't get away with it. You pulled one stroke too many. I volunteered to sort this out since I had to be in London this week, anyway.' One big hand closed over the other. 'That's you filled in. So what are you going to do to put matters right?'

'What do you expect me to do?' George squeaked. 'I've no money. I haven't a job so how can I have any money? As for the odds and ends of clothes I borrowed, they were threadbare. The boots needed re-heeled. I thought they were cast-offs . . .'

'You knew they weren't cast-offs. Don't hit me with the wide eyes and the same patter you used to oil your way into the company's wallets and wardrobes. I want to take the clothes back with me. Actors on the road can't afford to lose anything.'

'I haven't got any of the stuff,' George mumbled.

'How come?'

'I – I had to get rid of some things.'

'You flogged them?'

George shrugged.

'Then you'll pay for them.'

'I can't!'

'You'll have to find a way.'

George looked up at Colin, then at Chilton. 'Look, I've nothing – I don't even have a proper place to stay – '

'Tough.'

'But you're saying I have to pay up and I'm explaining to you that I can't.'

'Listen.' Chilton spread his hands a fraction. 'I've

promised people that you'll be *made* to make amends. Unlike you, I never hand out promises I don't keep. Now one way or another, you're going to cough up. Myself, I'd sooner beat the shit out of you, but for other people's sakes something more formal will have to be done. If you've no money, the government will help out. They always do. In return for the company waiving any action on your breach of contract, a lawyer will draw up a paper, making you agree to pay back what you owe in suitable instalments. If you welch on that you'll get nicked.' Chilton sat back. 'Where are you living?'

'He's at my place,' Colin said. He fumbled out a card and put it on the table in front of Chilton. 'That's only temporary, mind you.'

'It'll do.' Chilton looked at the card, then slipped it in his pocket. 'I'm in town for four more days. Time enough to get this business squared up.' He tapped the pocket where the card was. 'This'd better be on the level, by the way. If I have to hunt for this sod again it'll put me in a terrible mood.'

'It's kosher,' Colin said.

'Good. Tomorrow, then, we'll get your finances organized at the Social Security, then we'll – '

George moved so fast neither Colin nor Chilton had time to react. He cleared the edge of the table an instant before his beer hit Chilton's eyes. The shock sent Chilton backwards, scrambling to rise and to clear his vision. George knocked Colin aside as he raced to the door.

'George! Don't be so stupid! Come back!'

Colin put down his glass, getting ready to follow George. But he was pushed aside again as Chilton tore across the carpet and caught the door.

'Leave the bugger to me!' he growled, diving out on to the street.

Colin went to the other door and looked out. At first

he saw no one. The alley beside the pub was dark and lined with shadowy barrels and trash cans. Then there was a crash and he saw an arm go up in the air, then another.

'Don't! Please . . . No!'

George sounded terrified. There was scuffling, a bump and another crash as something metal hit the ground.

'Bloody heap of shit!'

Colin was moving before he knew it. He heard Chilton's grunting breath as he got near. A big arm came up against the lamplight from the street and dropped, connecting with a crack. George gurgled and whimpered.

'Get off! Leave him! He's no match for you!'

Colin gripped Chilton by the shoulder and pulled him away from George. For a frozen instant it seemed he would turn on Colin instead. But all he did was put a flattened hand on Colin's chest.

'I've no quarrel with you,' he panted. Beside him, out of sight in the shadows on the ground, George whimpered again. 'He'll pay back what he owes and he'll get a hammering into the bargain. As I see it, that's fair.'

'You've hammered him enough already.' With shaking hands Colin opened his coat and reached inside. 'Just tell me how much he owes. Tell me and I'll give it you, right now.'

Chilton remained motionless for a minute, gathering his breath. 'You must be off your crust,' he said.

'That's something for me to worry about,' Colin said. 'How much?'

'We worked it out at a hundred and thirty quid.'

Colin peeled off two fifties from the outside of his wad and three tens from the centre. He pushed them at Chilton.

'It's all there. Count it.'

'That won't be necessary.' Chilton tucked the money in

his pocket. 'I still think you're a mug. But thanks. This'll be returned to the people he owes.' Without looking at George again, he moved to the corner of the pub, buttoning his jacket. 'With a mate like that, you know you don't need enemies, don't you?'

Colin shrugged, not knowing if Chilton could see him clearly or not. He watched the big man turn and walk away.

'George. Are you all right?' He crouched, trying to make out George's shape.

'Oh sure, I'm all right.' George pushed himself up into the dim light, clutching his chest. 'A busted rib, by the feel of it, and half a dozen loose teeth. I'm great.'

'You asked for it, you know. That bloke was in the right. Maybe his sense of justice is a bit rough, but even so – '

'Spare me the sanctimony, will you?' George lurched away from the wall. 'Get me home. I want to clean myself up.'

'I don't know if you heard all that, but I squared things with him . . .'

'Yes,' George hissed, 'I heard, Colin. But do keep reminding me of it, won't you? You sure know how to get the edge on people.'

Colin turned, leading the way to where the car was parked. He was trying not to feel hurt. At the same time he was telling himself he asked for it, every bit as much as George did.

10

'I'm as ancient as me gums,' the old woman said, leaning on the side of Ena's bed, 'an' fifteen years older than me teeth. But they'll have a job gettin' rid of me, all the same.'

She was Sally Brampton. For five minutes she had been talking about her daughter and son-in-law, about the way they treated her as a nuisance about the house now that she spent most of her time in a chair in the living room. Sally believed she was a classic victim of an unpleasant modern syndrome called Granny Dumping. Old ladies, whenever they became too much of an obstacle – at Christmas-time and summer holidays – were often put in the hands of the medical authorities for two- and three-week periods, usually for trivial or trumped up reasons.

'They told the doctor I'd been gettin' out of bed an' wanderin' about at night. They said they was frightened I'd fall down the stairs. It's all codswallop. I sleep sound as a baby at night.'

There was proof enough of that. Old Sally's snores rattled through the ward night after night, putting an extra edge of misery on Ena's sleeplessness. Now, in daylight when drowsiness began to overtake her, she was being bombarded with Sally's woes. Hospital could be a terribly trying place.

'You should talk to the authorities about it,' Ena said. 'Get them to give your daughter and her husband a talking-to. If you're not sick you shouldn't be in here. There must be plenty of people with real illnesses needing your bed.'

'True enough.' Sally leaned one skinny hip against the bed and adjusted the angle of her walking stick. 'The thing that worries me worst, though, is maybe they'll do somethin' real nasty to me next time. That Barry, my son-in-law, he's a vicious devil. I wouldn't put it past him givin' me a shove at the top of the stairs. Just to get me out of the way for a month or two. Or for good.'

Ena was desperate for sleep. Her shoulder was throbbing, it had been since late last night. Sleep would be a welcome release from the hot, pounding ache. It would take her away from all that depressed her in this ward full of sick and moaning women. Why didn't old Sally go away and annoy somebody else?

'They'll be bringin' the tea round in a minute,' Sally said. 'I suppose I better get back to my bed. Them nurses don't like you goin' round socialisin', do they?'

Chance would be a fine thing, Ena thought. She had tried walking a couple of times, but as soon as she was upright the pain in her chest and shoulder had escalated sharply from ache to agony. So she was bed-bound, submitting to the indignity of bedpans and the recently added discomfort of sore patches on her shoulders, buttocks and heels.

But Sally was going. There was something. A bright plus in a miserable succession of minuses. Ena watched the old woman shuffle away. She wondered if she herself looked that frail and worn-out to other people. Probably she did. She certainly felt fragile and used-up, like a cracked, brittle, dry old twig.

She began to drowse. The ward and its sounds faded. Pain withdrew and light dreams crept forward. Ena saw her home, tidy and shining, warmly welcoming as she came in with two bulging bags of shopping. That was when her house was at its most likeable, on bright cold mornings when she had finished her shopping and came back to its embracing safety. No place like home. No place . . .

'Cup of tea, Mrs Russell?'

Ena came awake with a start. The nurse's voice had cut into her dream like a barbed knife.

'Tea, love?'

Ena clicked her tongue on her dry palate. 'I suppose I might as well have some, now you've wakened me.' No peace, she thought. No peace for the wicked. She'd never thought of herself as especially wicked. But there it was. No peace . . . 'Help me up in the bed a bit, will you?'

The nurse came to the bedside and grasped Ena's good arm.

'Take it gently now, Mrs Russell. Don't put any strain on that shoulder.'

Ena brought up her knees and dug her sore heels into the mattress. She pushed, inching herself up, panting softly with the effort.

'Easy now,' the nurse murmured. 'Easy . . .'

Ena's left heel slipped. She lurched on to her side.

'Aah! Ow!'

The nurse grabbed her, rolling her on to her back.

'Oh my God – it hurts! It hurts!'

'Sister!' the nurse yelled. She slid Ena squarely on to the pillows again, watching the change in her, seeing her lips turn blue as they drew back in a grimace of pain.

Sister came running. The nurse stepped back from the bed, seeing Ena's eyes roll back. Shock. She had seen it happen that way before. It was hardly surprising. As old Mrs Russell had rolled on her bad shoulder, there had been a buried, grating sound. That collar bone had gone again. The nurse was sure of it.

The sister stopped by the bed, took one swift look and told the nurse to fetch the doctor.

'Make it quick,' she said as the nurse hurried away.

On the bed Ena groaned once, softly, as consciousness slipped away from her.

The confusions and distractions of a busy morning gave way to abrupt annoyance, verging on anger, as Colin walked into the kitchen and saw the mess. Instant coffee powder had been spilled on the worktop and had solidified where it had landed on spilt water. A loaf was by the toaster, its wrapper open and three slices hanging out. A knife slicked with butter lay on the drainer and there was a glinting jewel of marmalade on the floor by the cooker. Blue wisps of toast-smoke hung in the air over the wash bowl, which was half full of grey greasy water.

Colin stumped through to the living room. George was in Ena's armchair, one leg swinging over the arm as he watched television. He had a plate in one hand and a wedge of toast in the other. His coffee cup was on the side table, where it had already made a couple of rings on the varnish.

'Just what the hell do you think this place is?'

George turned his head, eyebrows raised.

'You're turning it into a doss house.'

George swallowed a piece of toast and picked up his coffee mug. 'What's biting you now?'

'Everything. You move through this place like a muck spreader. That kitchen's a disgrace. And look at the mess you've made in here.' Colin pointed at a Coke can, a half empty crisp packet and a fanned-out bundle of magazines on the floor. 'This is my mother's living room, for God's sake. She'd have a fit if she saw it.'

George bit into the toast again. He chewed for a few seconds, looking about him.

'You're making too much of things,' he announced, spraying a few crumbs. 'The place just looks comfortably occupied. You were turning it into a mausoleum, sport.'

Colin gathered up the magazines, the can and the crisp packet. He slapped them on to the coffee table.

'I want you to sling that lot out, wipe the coffee drips off that table and get the kitchen cleaned up. And I don't want it done later. I want it done now.'

George sat up in the chair, staring. 'I don't remember signing any service contract, Colin. If you want a home help, go and hire one.'

Colin walked to the door and back again, a hand clamped on his forehead. 'How can you do this?'

'What?'

'Go into someone's home and treat it with such disrespect. I couldn't ever conduct myself this way. Don't you feel you've some responsibility towards me, towards my mother?'

Slowly, with studied timing, George got out of the chair. He took his plate and mug to the kitchen, came back and picked up the stuff from the table.

'You invited me to stay here, remember? I didn't come begging.'

'You asked me if I knew of anywhere you could stay. So I let you have the spare room. For which you haven't offered me any rent – '

'You knew I was broke!'

'You've made no effort to help yourself!'

'I don't happen to have all your fancy contacts, do I?'

'I worked for what I've got!' Colin yelled. 'I didn't sit around on my backside waiting for other people to do everything for me – and then abuse them when they did!'

'Right. I get the message.' George flounced to the door with his armful of magazines and paused. 'I'll be out of your house and your life by noon. Unless you'd like me to be gone earlier than that.'

Colin groaned. 'Never mind the petulant gestures, George. I'm not throwing you out. I'm asking you – '

'Telling me!'

'All right, telling you to be a bit more careful around the house. It won't be long before Mum's out of hospital. The place has got to be kept in half-decent nick.'

'If she's coming out soon,' George said airily, 'I might as well clear off now, so you can sterilize the place and get a coat of polish on everything.'

'I could use some help.'

'Do I take that to mean you're inviting me to stay, even though I'd sooner clear off?'

Colin wandered to the window and looked out. Why was his professional life so successful, so tightly on the up and up, while his private existence was such a downgrade mess? Was one the penalty he paid for the other? He knew that was a fanciful notion, positively daft, yet at times he suspected he was the victim of Divine book-keeping – for every profit a balancing loss or setback. In his early struggling days of learning his craft, his private life had been better.

'I'll get rid of this stuff,' he heard George say. 'Then I'll make a start on the kitchen.'

He's only staying because he's got nowhere else to go.

The voice of reason again, patiently sending out its messages, its warnings.

You give him shelter, food and money. That's all he stays with you for. He's amoral. He's incapable of love or affection for another human being.

True, Colin thought, all true. But it was also true that the thought of George leaving his life was as painful as knowing he was treacherous and negative.

'Weak,' Colin whispered. 'You're weak.'

He went back upstairs. On his drawing board there was a near-finished drawing of a Georgian house front. It was a hotel now, aiming for the conference trade. Colin's brief was to make it look the way it really looked, but without the telephone box on the corner, the lamp post near the front doors, an ill-placed row of bushes and a couple of crooked chimneys. It was almost a straight illustration job, except that he had to incorporate the picture into a letterhead, as well as an advertisement. It had begun as a pleasant job, but now it bored him. The trouble was it was too easy. His mind wandered. He liked jobs that trapped his entire attention.

But it had to be done. He got on to the stool and picked up the Rotring pen he had been using to do the fine lining on the windows. The tip was a fraction off the paper when the telephone rang. He narrowly missed putting a blob of indian ink on the paper. Reminding himself he should do something about getting a less disturbing warbler on the 'phone, he put down the pen again and picked up the receiver.

'Colin Russell.'

'Ah, Mr Russell . . .' The man at the other end cleared his throat. 'I'm Doctor Wilder, consultant physician at the hospital where your mother is. I don't believe we've met.'

'No, we haven't. Is something wrong?'

'I think you should come over to the hospital as soon as you can, Mr Russell.'

'What is it?' Colin was holding the receiver with both hands now.

'Your mother has, ah, taken a bit of a turn for the worse . . .'

'What does that mean?'

'If you'll just come over soonest, I'll talk to you then. It's best you be here, I think.'

Colin put down the receiver. He looked at the window, the walls. Was this it? Was the future he had tried to defer, in his mind at least, actually here?

He grabbed his jacket and went downstairs. George was in the kitchen, swabbing the worktop.

'I've got to go to the hospital . . .'

'Christ . . .' George frowned. 'You've gone white. Is something wrong?'

'I don't know. The guy wouldn't say much. Mum's taken a turn for the worse, that's all I know.' Colin zipped his jacket. 'I don't know how long I'll be. Look after things, eh?'

'Sure.'

It was less than a ten-minute drive. Colin parked behind the main hospital block and took the lift up to Women's Medical. As soon as he entered the ward a man approached him. He wore no white coat but he was obviously a doctor. He had the bearing, the controlled movements that fitted this environment.

'You'll be Mr Russell.'

'That's right,' Colin said, suddenly needing to swallow.

'I'm Doctor Wilder.'

'How's my mother?'

Wilder pointed to a door. It was the ante-room Colin had waited in before. 'Would you come in here, please?'

They went in and sat down, Wilder taking the chair behind the small table. He composed his arms as if he were about to deliver a lecture.

'I have to tell you,' he said, 'that your mother has died.'

The words did nothing to Colin. Rather, they seemed to take something away.

'It happened only a few minutes ago. I'm sorry you weren't here, but everything happened so quickly. She passed away peacefully, I can assure you of that.'

There was still nothing. Colin knew his mother was dead, but as a fact it didn't fit anywhere in his emotions. Something had happened to his whole emotional network.

'I've brought you in here,' Dr Wilder said, 'to explain what went wrong – you're entitled to know that, for I'm sure you expected no such development as this. No one did.'

'She – ' Colin heard his voice. He had to force himself to think what he meant to say. 'Was it the diabetes?'

'That played a major role. It had depleted her system. It weakened her resistance to injury – which resulted in her being here, of course. But diabetes, unstabilized, does so many other things to an old person's body. You know that, of course. I understand you've looked after your mother for a number of years.'

Now something *was* beginning to happen. Colin felt the sharp break in his line of expectation. He had come here to see his mother, to talk to her. But he couldn't, and wouldn't. What he would see instead would be lifeless and nothing to talk to. He remembered her last words to him: *Bring me the yellow bedjacket.*

'Are you all right, Mr Russell?' Wilder was leaning across the table, running a skilled eye across Colin's face. 'Would you like a drink of water, perhaps . . .'

'No, thanks. It's just beginning to hit me, I think . . .'

'Yes, well, this kind of news is hard to take in, immediately. Would you sooner wait awhile before I tell you what happened? Perhaps this is all a bit soon . . .'

'No, please go on,' Colin said. 'I think I need somebody to talk to.'

'I was saying how diabetes and associated conditions had weakened your mother's system. We noticed, after her first forty-eight hours here, that her responses to therapy were sluggish, and in some areas she showed no response at all. Even yesterday, she wasn't showing the kind of recovery level we would have expected in a woman of her age.'

'What happened today?'

'A simple movement, while she was still in bed, broke her collar bone again.'

'Oh my God.'

Colin pictured her pain and felt his heart flood with pity, then with unexpressed love. His throat swelled as he pulled out his handkerchief and pressed it to his face.

'Severe shock invaded a system that was already weak and under stress. We can't be sure yet, but there's a suspicion she may have suffered an embolism, because of the fracture . . .' The doctor sighed. 'A houseman and two nurses made a brave and sustained attempt to save her, but in the end she succumbed. It's no consolation to say this, Mr Russell, but you should know it all the same – I don't believe your mother would have survived long, anyway.'

Colin nodded. 'Her spirit had been drained,' he said. 'That was obvious to myself and my brother. But I had the feeling there would be some years left to her. I believed it because it's what I hoped . . .'

'Yes, quite.'

The nerve-baring sensations were setting in. Colin felt the swelling of grief, the heart-tearing acceptance of a truth almost too monstrous to face. *His mother was dead.* The centre of his life had been scooped out. He felt a tear move down his cheek.

'There will be things to do, of course,' Wilder said, almost apologetically. 'Catastrophe has a way of turning into paperwork. If you need any help or guidance, there's a social worker here who'll be glad to lighten the load.'

'The first thing I should do is tell my brother.'

'Do you want to use our telephone?'

Colin thought about it, then nodded. 'Yes, if I could.'

Dr Wilder took him along to Sister's room. When Colin was alone he called Bill's number in Devon, fully expecting to speak to his sister-in-law, Eunice. But it was Bill himself who answered.

'Bill, I'm calling from the hospital . . .'

Colin listened to the anxiety in his brother's voice.

'Mum's passed away.'

Bill was silent. Colin waited, saying nothing. When the questions finally came he answered the ones he could. They arranged to meet; Bill could be in London by evening. By the time he hung up, Colin knew his brother was crying, even though he had tried to hide it.

There was no question of going straight home. Colin recoiled from the thought of stepping into his mother's house and knowing she would never be there again. He drove to a place in the West End where he knew, or was pretty sure he knew he'd find a trace of solace. He sat behind the lettered glass of a coffee shop window and waited. At a little after noon Mandy Riley came in. The thoughtful, frowning look left her face the instant she saw Colin.

'What are you doing here?' She came over and kissed his cheek.

'I remembered you're a creature of habit. You've been using this place at about this time every weekday for a couple of years now, haven't you?'

'Smart work, Sherlock. I was thinking about phoning you, only the other day. Just to find out how you were.'

'I was a lot better than I am now,' Colin said.

'Why? What's wrong?'

He told her. She sat down and clasped his hands.

'I'm not after a shoulder to cry on,' he said. 'I suddenly had a need for someone I trusted, someone I could be with while the pain sets in. Selfish of me, of course. I'll probably ruin your break.'

'Silly,' Mandy said, giving his hands a tight squeeze before she released them. 'It's great to see you. I'm only sorry it took something so sad, so terrible, to make you come and see me.'

It was the greatest of oddities, Colin thought, but it was a fact: he was never more calm nor more confident of himself than when he was with Mandy. She felt practically the same way about him. Yet it was a relationship devoid of the usual man-woman chemistry.

'Do you want to talk about your mother?' Mandy said.

'No. I need to think about her. A lot. But not talk. What I want to do right now is drink a few cups of good coffee with you, draw whatever it is I draw from you, and hear how your life's going – as long as it's going better than the last time we met.'

'If you hadn't come to me that time, when I asked you to,' Mandy said, 'I think my life would be the pits by now. But you did come to my rescue . . .'

'Did it really amount to as much as that? Rescue?'

'You better believe it. I did what you said I should. I stayed clear of contact, clear of disaster. But more important than that, I took your programming advice.'

'The terribly hard advice.'

'The *murderously* hard advice,' Mandy said. 'But you were right. It changes a person. Trying to hurt nobody makes it possible to like yourself, occasionally. I realized I hadn't been too fond of myself.'

'So you're happy?'

'To quote this bloke I know, I'm as happy as somebody like me can be.'

'Is there a man?'

Mandy shook her head. 'That'll happen when it happens. I'm not going to force anything.'

'You'll be fine,' Colin said. 'I might even write you an airtight guarantee.'

They sat looking at each other. Coffee came, they drank some, then looked at each other again.

'The pain's eating you, isn't it?' Mandy said.

'You can tell?'

'Yes. But stay. Take what you need from our time together. There'll be time enough for suffering on your own.'

11

Following the service at the crematorium the mourners, ten in all, returned to the house in Ealing to sip sherry, nibble ham sandwiches and talk. The conversations were mainly about Ena and the old days, trailing off inevitably into what the mourners themselves had been doing since they last saw one another.

Habit had taken Colin into the kitchen where he stood with his back to the drainer, nursing his drink, feeling and looking awkward in his dark suit and black tie. Bill stood beside him, chewing a sandwich as if it was plasticine.

'I hate funerals,' he said. 'Not that they're meant to be enjoyed. But everybody's so reluctant, aren't they? They don't really want to be here because death's something they'd rather not acknowledge.'

'Do you know what's getting to me?' Colin said. 'The cremation.'

'Well, that's understandable . . .'

'It means Mum doesn't exist any more. Not even her body. She's not in the world.'

'She's memories now, Colin.'

'That's for sure. Just memories. The trouble with me is, I remember best the things that should be forgotten. These last few days I've been crippling myself with guilt. I keep remembering the times I left her on her own when she wanted to stay in. Then there's all the little neglects, the harsh words . . .'

Bill gave Colin's shoulder a sharp squeeze. 'It'll pass. The memories will get gentler.'

'I'll try not to hurry the process,' Colin murmured. 'I'll do my full penance. I think it's due.'

In the living room Ena's cousin Bella, who hadn't been heard from in years, was telling a brother-in-law from Putney about the times she and Ena used to go cycling as girls. Further across the room two elderly male half-cousins and a middle-aged niece were discussing the shockingly short, almost abrupt funeral service and the vicar's distant manner. An old friend of Ena's husband, a man who had kept in touch sporadically over the years, stood alone by the window, staring out at the street.

Aunt Joan and cousin Elaine were wandering round the room, running an inventory.

'That vase,' Joan said, 'was a wedding present from your father. I always said to Ena I'd like to have it, if anything happened.'

'She'll have made a proper will, of course,' Elaine said. 'She was always saying people should make wills. I think you'll find the lot goes to Colin and Bill.'

Joan pursed her mouth sourly. 'I don't think that would be very fair.'

'Nothing in life's particularly fair, mother.' Elaine stepped close to a watercolour reproduction on the wall by the door. She frowned at it. The scene was the front at Weston-Super-Mare, on one of those rare days when the sea is visible. 'What a terrible little daub.'

'I gave Ena that,' Joan said.

'Oh. I suppose it's got a certain charm – it's just not my taste, that's all.' Elaine looked at her mother. 'What are you doing?'

Joan was craning her neck, trying to look through to the kitchen without making herself seen.

'I wonder what those two are cooking up through there.'

'They'll be talking about their mother, I suppose.'

'Mm. Maybe. I want to have a word with Colin. There's things should get sorted out, while we're here.'

'What things?'

'Family matters.'

As Joan spoke Colin and Bill came out of the kitchen. Bill went to the sideboard to get himself a drink. Colin looked at the people in the living room as if he was surprised, faintly, to see them there.

'Colin,' Joan said in a low voice, 'could I have a word?'

'Of course.'

Joan looked pointedly at Elaine, who got the signal and moved off.

'There's one or two things Ena said to me, over the past couple of years, and I want to let you know, while we're here, since we're not likely to be seeing too much of each other from now on.'

Colin nodded slowly. 'What kind of things, Auntie?'

'Oh . . .' Joan fluttered her hand, dismissing the possibility that she had anything serious to tell him. 'Ena had some things she said she wanted me to have, that's all.'

'So you want to talk about Mum's *things* – not about things she said?'

'Well, you could put it like that, I suppose . . .'

Colin looked at the old man by the window. Of all the people there, other than brother Bill, that man seemed to carry the same burden of loss Colin did. He was hunched and beaten looking, willing his feelings far out beyond their dismal gathering.

'I think it's only right,' Joan went on, 'especially when we're talking about the wishes of the dead . . .'

'The dead haven't got wishes,' Colin said. 'The dead haven't got anything.'

'You know what I mean,' Joan snapped.

'Well go on, then. What is it you want to say?'

Joan shifted her handbag from one wrist to the other.

'Your mother had a bracelet, it was silver and jade, nothing terribly valuable but a pretty thing . . .'

'She used to wear it at Christmas.'

'And it had a matching necklace. I think your father gave them to her. Well there's those and a gold brooch, shaped like a leaf with a tiny little diamond on it . . .'

'I know the brooch,' Colin said. 'Dad gave her that, too.'

'And she'd a pair of crocodile shoes, not new by any means, but we took the same size, Ena and me . . .'

'So what about these things?'

'Your mother told me I could have them. There's a vase, too, that one over there, and – '

'That's enough!' Colin hissed.

Joan took a step back from him. She looked as if she'd been struck.

'My mother is dead. We're here to mourn her passing. I am, at any rate.'

'And so am I,' Joan said indignantly.

'Then you'll forgive me for thinking you're here for the sole purpose of grabbing what you can get while you can.'

'How dare you!'

'Lower your voice, Aunt Joan, or I'll have to ask you to leave,' Colin stepped close. 'For the record, I don't believe, for one second, that Mum said you could have anything. She wasn't the kind who sat around making pronouncements about how she'd like her property divided. I think you told her you liked certain things she owned, and that was all. To some people, saying they fancy something is tantamount to sticking in an early claim.'

'If your mother could hear what you're saying to me – '

'Maybe she can,' Colin said. 'I don't believe it, myself, but it's a soothing thought. And if she *can* hear, she'll be pleased I'm keeping plunderers away from the things she valued.'

Joan flounced away as Bill approached.

'What was she squeaking about?'

'She was trying a spot of grave robbing. I warned her off.'

'Old cow,' Bill murmured. 'I've never liked her.' He glanced at the old man by the window. 'Charlie's taking Mum's death pretty bad, by the look of him.'

'Yeah. I don't remember him too well, although Mum talked about him quite a bit. He always got a Christmas card, too.'

'He was an admirer.'

'Really?'

Bill nodded. 'It was all totally innocent, but I think he must have fancied Mum for a long, long time. There were signs, things I remember from the time I was a little kid.' He smiled. 'It's got a lot of charm, that kind of situation.'

'I think I'll have a word with him,' Colin said. 'He's been getting ignored.'

'Before you do, let me just tell you this – I might not have time later, what with my train leaving at three and all the goodbyes I'll have to say.' Bill took a folded letter from his pocket, tapped it, and put it away again. 'That's confirmation from head office that I can have an area transfer. Do you remember one night at the hospital, I said I'd something I wanted to talk to you about?'

'Yes, I've wondered about it a time or two.'

'I'm coming back to London,' Bill said. 'I'll never be settled, in my head anyway, until I'm back. I'm not a country boy at heart – and there are other reasons. I mentioned them to you. Eunice's in favour of the move, and I think a London schooling would be better for the kids.'

'When's this going to happen?'

'Not before next year. The guy who handles the inner London area retires in February. I'll take over his patch. What I'd been planning to do was try to buy a house round here, as near to this road as I could. Now – well, I don't know how you'll feel about what I'm going to say.'

'Try me.'

'We're going to be joint owners of this house, once the documentation's put in order. I wondered how you'd feel about me buying out your half, so me and the wife and kids can make this our home.'

Colin thought about it. 'Right at the moment I don't know how I feel, Bill. I'd vaguely pictured myself going on living here.' Colin smiled. 'You really want to be back where it all started, don't you?'

'There's nothing I want more,' Bill said.

'I suppose, when I look at it straight, there's no point in me living alone in a house this size. I'd be better off in a flat. I've got used to this being home, though.'

'Let's not talk about it any more. We'll leave it till later. I've given you something to think about, when you're up to it. Go and talk to Charlie.'

The old man was consulting his big silver pocket watch when Colin approached him.

'Charlie,' he said, 'I'm sorry you've been neglected. Can I get you a drink or a sandwich or something?'

'No thanks, son.' The soft-lined face creased into a smile. It was a face quite out of its time, the type that adorned old sepia snapshots, kind and hopelessly innocent. 'I'm at a time of life when I get by on very little. And today I don't feel like eating or drinking.'

'It was good of you to come,' Colin said. 'I know Mum thought highly of you.'

'And she was never far from my thoughts.'

'You should have visited more. She'd have loved to see you.'

'I thought about it a lot, after your dad passed on. But I decided it wouldn't be right. I wrote, though, and I always got an answer.' Charlie gazed through the window for a moment. 'It's more than twenty years since I saw Ena, did you know that? But I've kept her picture fresh in my mind.' He looked at Colin. 'Old bachelors live with more dreams than reality,' he said.

Hours later, Colin sat alone in his mother's bedroom, finding echoes in the simplest of her belongings. If there was a final moment of goodbye, he believed he had come to it. The shape she had imposed on the room, the arrangement of bed, wardrobe, dressing table, chairs, mirrors and pictures, was about to be cancelled forever. The boxes were waiting on the landing. The sooner the job of packing them was tackled, the sooner Colin would feel he had put her properly to rest.

At five o'clock, as he was leaning the rolled carpet on the stacked furniture along one side of the room, the telephone rang. He went downstairs and answered it.

'Colin. It's George.'

Something different in the voice, he thought. Something guarded.

'Hi. It's all over. I've just finished clearing Mum's room. You can come back any time you feel like it.' George had diplomatically withdrawn that morning, just as he had done when Bill came to the house the night Ena died. 'I don't feel like cooking anything,' Colin went on. 'I thought we might go out and have a bite.'

There was even something different about the pause.

'Are you still there, George?'

'Yes, yes. Listen Colin, why don't you come over to Kilburn? There's a great bar here where they sell food in the evening.'

Kilburn? 'What are you doing in Kilburn?'

'Visiting with a friend. Somebody I met at my agent's a

while back. We met up again this morning when I looked in at the office. We had a few lunchtime jars in the pub I'm talking about. It's old and very stylish. You'll love it.'

'Can you give me directions, then?'

Colin drew the pad towards him and flipped the cap off the pen. As George explained the route he began to write, thinking: something's afoot. Something I'm not going to like.

The first thing he didn't like was the pub. For a start it wasn't old, or the interior wasn't. It was a fibreglass, plastic and fake-brass replica of a Victorian pub – the brewery's idea of a Victorian pub, which was wildly at odds with the real thing. From the Dralon curtains and over-warm lighting to the formica bar top and leatherette seating, the place was a nightmare of bad taste and worse design.

Identities were hard to make out in the reddish light. It darkened eyes and diluted features. People looked artificial, matching the artificiality of their surroundings. Colin walked along the bar, trying not to stare. He found George leaning on the curved corner by the infra-red food servery. He was with a tall thin man who, allowing for the effect of the lighting, must have been about forty. He stared with a trace of hostility as Colin approached and touched George's arm.

'Ah!' George registered bright cordiality. 'You made it.'

'It was easier than I thought,' Colin said, swiftly gauging the other man's appearance and coming up with a word to fit: reptilian.

'Colin . . .' George stepped back to make the introductions. 'Meet Donald.'

Colin put out his hand. 'How do you do.' He felt

Donald's fingers close aggressively on his own, then withdraw sharply.

'Colin's a graphic designer,' George went on brightly. 'He does absolutely super stuff. Really going places, aren't you, Colin?'

'If you say so. What do you do, Donald?'

'I'm a theatrical agent.' It was said with the special hush and distance people in enviable professions sometimes used when they announced their credentials. 'I handle mainly TV work these days, though. One has to go where the real money is.'

'Oh. Fascinating.'

George flashed a fiver. 'What'll you have, Colin?'

'No, no,' Colin protested, 'I'll get them in.'

'Both of you keep your hands in your pockets,' Donald said, pulling out a roll. 'What'll it be, Colin?'

Colin said he'd like a pint of bitter. The sense he'd had earlier, of something impending, something unpleasant, was stronger now. George was putting on an act and Donald was doing a stand-off. Colin was beginning to feel very bad. After a couple of hours clearing his mother's room, he needed George's comfort and his companionship. He didn't believe it was forthcoming. But something else was.

'Donald works in collaboration with my agent a lot of the time,' George said as the drinks were served up.

'I put business his way,' Donald said, swaying his head as he spoke, enhancing the snake-like appearance. 'I think I must be sentimental. There's certainly not much profit in it for me.'

'Do you handle any big names?' Colin said.

'Well.' Donald drew himself up. When he spoke again he seemed to address the air above Colin's head. 'It depends what you call a big name. I mean there are talentless trolls around the business with names that everyone knows. But I don't call them big names. I go in for *durable* names. People who may not be stars, but who will last.'

'I see.' Colin found it disconcerting that the man wouldn't look at him when he spoke. 'How about our George here? Is he going to be one of the durable people?'

'His talent, I believe, has been mismanaged. Frankly it hasn't been managed at all. Given the right exposure, in the right direction, I'd say yes, he'll be a durable actor.'

'Chuck it,' George said, grinning. 'My head's big enough as it is.'

'The truth will out,' Donald said, widening his eyes at George. The eyes had a possessive look as they flicked for a second to Colin. 'I'm not noted for making bad judgements.'

Colin's stomach shifted as George squeezed Donald's wrist. It was a fleeting, light-as-air gesture, but it was heavy with meaning. The voice of reason spoke:

You've been brought here to see this, to be told by acts instead of words. To get the hint and take it. You've lost George.

'So will you be taking George on as a client?'

Colin saw the snake eyes harden and felt glad he had landed a punch. Not that it would do him any good. But he wasn't going down with a shrug. He was hurting too much for that.

'There would be difficulties in taking him on,' Donald said, his eyes on the space over Colin's head again.

'Oh?'

'Dear me, yes. There's such a thing as loyalty, as I'm sure you've heard.' A thin smile tempered the crack. The bitching was underway.

'I thought loyalty was a thing of the past,' Colin said, darting a look at George.

'There's always the misplaced kind, of course,' Donald retorted. 'The nonsense loyalties, the loyalties based on independence, for example.' Again, fleetingly, the possessive eyes. 'I'm referring to proper loyalties, such as the kind George has to his agent. He can't just throw that aside, any more than I can breach it.'

'But wouldn't he be better off being handled professionally by somebody like you – somebody with such faith in his potential?'

Go on, Colin thought, admit it, snake face. You wouldn't represent an unreliable, undisciplined loser like George Packer.

'The contractual difficulties would be horrendous, even if we were to set loyalty aside.' Donald yawned pointedly. 'I hate talking shop,' he said, addressing George. 'I hate hanging about too long in pubs, too. Fancy going on somewhere else?'

'Yes,' George said, 'why not?'

Colin felt the exclusion like a fist on his chest. He wasn't being invited. He wasn't wanted. The important message had been delivered and now he was nothing more than a pest.

George turned, his eyes already distant. 'I suppose you'll have things to do, Colin.' He buttoned his jacket, an overture to swift departure.

'Well, since I've only just got here,' Colin said, 'I might as well stop and have some plastic grub.' Knowing how pathetic it would sound, how stupidly forlorn, he couldn't stop himself adding, 'I'll see you later on, eh?'

'Um . . .' George looked at Donald, then at the floor. 'I won't be coming back tonight. Got something planned.'

'Oh, I see. Tomorrow, then. '

'Well, look, to tell you the truth . . .' George paused as Donald swept away from the bar, nodding a cold goodbye to Colin. 'I'm going to move out, mate. I know I've been in the way, so I've made the effort and I've got a place to stay.'

Colin jerked his head at the door, where Donald was waiting. 'With him?'

'Yes, that's right. Just for the time being. I'll be round in the morning to get my things. I'll let myself in early but I won't disturb you. You'll find my key on the hall table.'

Colin wanted to say something, but George slapped his arm and moved away before anything came into his head.

He stayed and finished his drink, then went to the lavatory and was violently sick. When he had cleaned himself up he left the pub, got into the car and came to the very edge of despairing tears.

But they didn't come. A renegade spark flared in him, holding him steady. He gripped the wheel and set his teeth. *They won't break me. Nothing will.*

He drove home slowly, watching the people on the streets as he passed. He wondered at the pain there must be out there, pain and emptiness as severe as his own – and none of it showing. Human suffering was like an iceberg. You never saw more than a fraction.

'Bloody world . . .'

Here he was, sitting behind the wheel of his car, driving with care, outwardly the most self-possessed of men. How many more were there? Who knew what miseries were tearing at calm, blank-faced people out there on the pavements? There *had* to be more like him, holding themselves together in spite every reason to give in to whimpering despair.

So he was trying to conjure fellowship with strangers on the streets. So why not? Grief, especially when it was double bladed, could perhaps be endured if he made himself believe he wasn't the only victim.

When he let himself into the house the first thing he saw was George's coat hanging on a peg. Another echo.

Colin hung up his own coat and went into the living room. He switched on the side light and looked at his mother's empty chair.

Whispering, he said, 'I'm home, Mum.'

He patted the arm of the chair, not feeling at all foolish for enacting this small fantasy. Earlier, standing there by the window, he had taken poor sad Charlie's words to heart: 'Old bachelors live with more dreams than reality.'

12

The week before Christmas Colin had a call from brother Bill. The deal over the house, Bill said, had gone through. What he meant was that he had sold his house in Devon; the appropriate sum from the proceeds would soon be deposited in Colin's bank account. It then only remained for Colin to sign the agreement to surrender his half of the house in Ealing.

'I can hardly wait,' Bill said. 'I go to bed thinking about it and I dream about it and I wake up remembering the dream – me, back home, living in the old house. I can't tell you how it feels, Colin. It's like waiting for a birthday when I was a kid.'

'I'm pleased for you, Bill.'

'And I'm pleased you decided it would be OK for us to have the house. I'm delighted. There was a time when I thought you might be sticky over the idea.'

'I was reluctant to face the notion of moving out,' Colin said. 'But like I told you in September, that's all changed.'

'Well don't go changing your mind before you sign that bit of paper,' Bill said, only half joking.

'If you like, I'll sign another bit of paper promising I won't change my mind.'

Bill laughed. They talked some more about the house move, then about Christmas, when Colin would spend three days with his brother and his family in Devon. Just before he hung up, Bill said he would be waiting at the station when Colin arrived in five days' time, so he wasn't to worry about getting a taxi.

Not long after the 'phone call the post arrived. There

was a Christmas card from one of Colin's clients, a diary from another and a letter on good quality beige paper, inviting him to a farewell party, that very day. He looked at the date on the envelope. It had taken four days to get to him, even though it had a first class stamp and had been posted less than five miles away. He would have been sad if it had arrived late. Much as farewells saddened him, this was one he didn't want to miss.

For an hour he worked on a new commission, a promotional trade brochure for an obscure, expensive malt whisky. The company wanted to avoid the heather-and-hillside image with their product. Rather, they wanted to sell their scotch to the chic set, the people who placed great store by fashion and considered price unimportant, as long as it was high.

Colin had put the name of the drink in noble, elongated, stylish roman letters across the top of the brochure cover. Beneath was a picture of a strong male hand holding a chunky, pricey-looking glass half full of something that looked like liquid amber. The key to the illustration, the up-market selling point, was the man's wrist, where a fraction of a gold Rolex Oyster's dial peeked from the edge of an immaculate shirt cuff.

'Pure illusion,' Colin murmured.

He sat back and appraised the effect. The lie told by the picture was nearly perfect. Men with hands like that didn't wear Rolex watches. It was a worker's hand, perhaps a fighter's, with taut sinews and fingers made powerful from constant strain. An attractive hand, a hand belonging to someone with power that was apparent on sight. The kind of man who wore that shirt and that watch would be more likely to have a hand without character, under-used and rather flabby. But the illusion worked. It was a dream, the desirable made almost real.

'The story of my life.'

Colin decided it was time to get ready for the party. He covered his artwork, switched off the lamp and went through to his bedroom. Another illusion, he thought, looking at the stark white walls and the few carefully chosen pictures, the lacquered chest, knee-high bookcase and slim black wardrobe. He had shaped this place to suit the man he would have liked to be. It was hard to live up to, an occasionally unsettling place to lie down in.

He decided on a pair of mid-grey slacks, freshly dry-cleaned and expertly pressed. They betokened care and a degree of conservatism, neatly softened by the navy-blue polo neck sweater and pepper-and-salt jacket. It was more illusion building, but Colin saw no harm in it, really. An image protected a person, and at times he felt very much in need of such protection.

The party was in a reception room at a publisher's, a room designed for parties, mainly book launches. There were tables with white covers by the windows and along two walls. Some food had been provided – little savoury biscuits, dainty oblong sandwiches and various dips that looked like fresh, garish oil paint. But drink was much more in evidence. As soon as Colin arrived a glass of white wine was thrust into his hand; he was told to get it down him and help himself to more whenever he felt like it.

He wandered through the crowd without being noticed, feeling casually excluded. The people were daunting. They spoke in chirrups, laughed aggressively and bandied smart remarks. They were firmly centred in versions of themselves that they wanted to project at other people.

Why, Colin wondered, did illusion seem so evident today? He noticed it in everything, even in the way the security man on the door, as he came in, had used his uniform and a scowl to suggest he was something more formidable than he really was.

'Hello, Colin.'

He turned and saw someone devoid of illusion. Mandy looked precisely herself.

'Thank God you found me,' Colin said. 'I was beginning to think I'd be forced to trot out my only three quips.'

'And what are they?'

'Let's see – oh yes. If somebody says I'm not looking too well, I say I'm only lugging my body around for its sentimental value.'

Mandy laughed.

'And if I see somebody I want to chat up, I say, Excuse me, I'm a stranger around here – could you direct me to your house? The third one's a definition. Memory's what you forget with.'

'I'll stick close and make sure you don't have to tussle with any of the crowd,' Mandy promised.

She led Colin to a corner on the edge of the crowd. There was a table where they could put down their drinks and an ashtray where Mandy could flick her ash.

'There. We can have our own private party.'

Colin nodded at the others. 'They must think a lot of you, to throw a bash like this for your leave-taking.'

'It's a two-in-one. This is a farewell party and the Christmas do rolled into one.' Mandy sipped her drink and winked. 'What do you make of my news, then?'

'I'm pleased. And sad.'

'I'm kind of sad, too. But if somebody walked in here and told me the deal's off, I'd be mad as hell.'

'Why America?' Colin said.

'Because it's still the land of opportunity. One of its opportunities was practically dropped in my lap, and I knew I'd have been a mug not to take it.'

'Any other reason?'

Mandy smiled. 'You *are* a mindreader. Yes, of course there is. I want to put the old life squarely behind me.

I've known for a while I need a new start. It's like wiping the slate, Colin. I'm going to start over, in practically every way, and this time I'm going to get it right.' She stubbed out her cigarette. 'That affair took more out of me than I thought. I got over it, but I was suffering from drag, if you get what I mean.'

'Oh yes, I get you, all right. I'm embarking on a new start myself. For reasons much the same as yours, though I'm not actually going to leave the country. Just the old scene.'

'When?'

'Some time in the New Year. I'm moving out of the house and going to work with a design team on a project in Birmingham for a few weeks. After that, I'm going to buy myself a flat. I fancy moving into the East End.'

'Ooh.' Mandy raised her eyebrows. 'Very trendy, Colin. It's definitely the in thing to do.'

'I like the East End. That's my reason, it's got nothing to do with what's trendy. The people are real. Not too many illusions floating about.'

'Won't you miss Ealing?'

Colin shook his head firmly. 'No. It's been the scene of too much pain for me. Too much turmoil.' He hesitated, half reluctant to say what he wanted to say. 'I – well, I had one particularly bad emotional wrench, earlier in the year. It happened at the time Mum died, so my resistance was low. Instead of getting over it properly I got drag, like you did. Maybe worse. I could go about my business, feeling everything was all right. I met other friends and got along with them well enough. But then I'd see someone like the person I'd lost, or hear a voice that was the same, and that was enough to bring me to girlish tears.'

'And it's still bad?'

'Yes, it is,' Colin said. 'By the time September came

round I realized the condition was chronic. I could handle it, but I knew a change of scene, a change of outlook, would help me to handle it better. So I decided to tell my brother he could buy me out of the house. He wanted to do that anyway.'

'Happy ever after, then?'

'I'm not sure what happy is,' Colin said. 'I wonder if I've ever really known. When I try to think of happy times, what I remember are times when things were less unhappy – times when my life was different, but not necessarily happy.'

Mandy punched his arm softly. 'Watch it. This is a party, remember. You're going sombre on me.'

'Sorry.' Colin kissed her cheek and raised his glass. 'Here's to you, my love. All the best for the future.'

'All the best to you, Colin.'

They drank and kissed again.

'I think we should join the fray,' Mandy said. 'A bit of mindless revelry's good for the spirit.'

'Whatever you say. But stick close, in case I run out of quips.'

It was getting dark when Colin left the building, having spent a final, none-too-sober ten minutes alone with Mandy, leaning on a railing overlooking the stair well. They exchanged promises to keep in touch and to stick to their programming. They said how much they would miss being able to get in touch as easily as they had in the past. In the end Mandy had become weepy and Colin had comforted her, feeling tearful himself.

Now, out in the cold, suddenly remembering where he had put the car, he stood on the edge of the pavement and wondered what he could do with the rest of the evening, sooner than go back to the house.

'Merry Christmas, mate,' one of the revellers called, coming out of the doors behind Colin.

'Merry Christmas.'

A couple of kindly words could do wonders, Colin thought, warmed by the greeting. If a person put himself on a strict emotional diet, he could get by on a minimum of human warmth and generosity.

He smiled, gazing up at the darkening sky. As long as he preserved enough illusion, he decided, a change of scene and a change of diet would very likely see him through.